UNWRITTEN

HATTIE JUDE

Unwritten
by Hattie Jude

ISBN-13: 978-1-7335137-7-7

Cover by Jena Brignola
Editing: Christine Estevez
hattiejude@gmail.com

CHAPTER ONE

It's a fresh hell every time I step foot into the halls of a new school. In the past, everyone has known who I am before I ever get there, and they already have a preconceived idea of who they think I'll be. I've been called every name in the book: snot, brown-noser, suck-up, stuck-up, fuck-up, bitch, slut, fake, princess, fake princess...insert foul name here. I've been in three public schools, a brief stint with homeschool, and we're giving an elite private school a chance this go around.

What makes it different this time is that I'm across the country. We said goodbye to our home in sunny Las Vegas and are trying out Long Island. I didn't expect my parents to agree on anything after their divorce, but my dad owes me, and as long as he stays far from me and my mom and pays for Longlake Academy, I'm okay.

I frown as I put on the new uniform. It's not the most flattering thing I've ever worn, but it'll be nice not to think about what to wear every day. Seems like the most elite school on the East Coast could've come up with something better than this navy and green pleated skirt, white shirt, and navy blazer.

If this uniform helps me blend in though, I'm all for it. A new school in a new town has me nervous enough. Having parents in the porn business is something I wouldn't wish on my worst enemy. You'd think with the highest grossing director in the porn industry for a father and the highest paid female porn star for a mother, they'd be lenient with me, but it's the opposite. Since the divorce and my mom's retirement, my mom is more controlling than ever. She's on some twisted quest for me to have a more wholesome upbringing. Too little, too late, Ma.

I'm willing to put up with it a little longer as I count down the days until I get into Columbia.

If I can just get through senior year at Longlake.

Fingers are crossed that no one will know who I am.

A girl can dream.

There's a stretch of time that I call *Before*...before I had my parents' utmost trust...before I lost my virginity...before I naively thought one of their coworkers actually had feelings for me...

Before.

Everything since Luke is *After.*

And the After has been a roller coaster. I thought with my father out of the picture, things would improve with my mother and me, but she's driving me crazy working overtime in the parental department.

She's in the kitchen with an egg-white omelet with vegan cheese and hot sauce on the table for me. She frowns when she sees me and I know it's coming. The rants will be starting extra early now that I have to go to school at the crack of dawn.

"Little heavy on the makeup, Jos...I mean, Gabriela.

You need to wash off about ninety percent of that. This isn't Vegas."

"How about you leave your makeup advice for one of your old co-stars and let me look how I want for my first day of school?" I take a few bites of the food and push back. "Thank you for breakfast."

"Aren't you going to finish that?"

"What and get fatter than I already am, according to you? I think I'll save that argument for another week."

"*Gabriela*." She sighs heavily like she's the grieved one, but we both know I can't do anything right with her these days. My hair, my heavy makeup, my attitude...last week, she yelled at me for breathing wrong. Apparently, I was huffing a little too much for her satisfaction and she was *fed up*.

Ever since I got out of rehab, she's been equal parts proud and ashamed of me. She praises me for my accomplishments but rips me apart for my appearance. I'm just trying to get through the day without turning to the vodka I know she still keeps locked in the dining room cabinet.

I do like our new McMansion. It's way too much house for the two of us, but we can go an entire day without running into each other. Small victories. As I do the loop around our circular driveway, then head down the rest of the long pavement, I admire the trellis of flowers on the side fence. I was sad to leave my succulent garden in Vegas, not to mention the warm weather, but a part of me is excited to have seasons and the challenge of growing things in a different environment than I'm used to.

I pull out of the gate and my stereo makes a loud, staticky sound that makes me jump. The honk puts a holy fear in me and I screech on the brakes, coming *this close* to hitting the car backing out of the driveway next door.

Things suddenly screech to slow motion. Speaking of breathing wrong, I think I just lost my air. The person in the other car is the most beautiful guy I've seen even with the rage he clearly feels toward me right now. I take a deep breath and mouth *Sorry* with a wave. When his expression doesn't change, I motion for him to go ahead. Since we're this close to one another, with me pulling forward out of the driveway and him backing out of his, I can see his jaw tick. His eyes are the color of a Siberian husky—that weird shade of icy blue-green—and when he glares at me, he looks like a fallen angel.

Maybe this is what all hot guys look like in Long Island, vicious and sculpted. I appreciated the guys in Vegas, but they didn't look like they wanted to reach out and pluck me out of the car and eat me for dinner.

My mouth falls open and I swear he seems to read all the lunatic thoughts I'm having because he lifts his shoulder in a barely-there acknowledgment and I want to hide below the dashboard.

I will have a lot to write about in my journal tonight.

When he eventually starts moving, I do the same, trying to focus on the road—something I should have been doing all along—and not lusting after *hot neighbor guy*. He makes a left turn sooner than I need to, but it doesn't stop me from obsessing. Thoughts of him distract me on the drive to school, so when I pull into the parking lot a few minutes later, I'm not doing the gross clammy sweat thing that seems typical of a first day of school, but I do feel a little overheated. Definitely better than gross clammy sweat.

I grab my bag and take my time before getting out, trying to think of a fitting mantra for the day. Laura, my new sponsor, is all about mantras. My mom has them posted all over the house. Laura seems great, but we'll have to work on her lines.

"You've got this."

"New day, new opportunity."

"What doesn't kill you makes you stronger..."

They're all a bit weak, like a second cup of tea with a used tea bag, and I don't feel any more positive than I did before saying them. I look in the mirror, smiling, and give an old mantra my twist. *"It's probably going to be a shit day, so just get through it one step at a time."* I wink at myself because I'm a geek who talks to herself and then acknowledges it, and maybe Laura is onto something because I do feel better.

Even though I open my door slowly, the wind is strong. I don't have a strong grip and the thud into the car door next to mine makes me yelp. *No.*

I hurry out of the car, my hand over my mouth as I hold back my squeaks of horror. I see the shoes first and then look up, up, up. I'm on the shorter side, but he's extremely tall and now he's looking at me like he wants to filet me over a grill and stick a stake through me. *Hot neighbor guy.*

I groan inside and then hold my hand out in an effort to be friendly.

"I'm...Gabriela Sinclair and I am so sorry."

My mom decided I should go by my middle name. My parents have the clever business names of Sookie Lane and Hugh Jerod so I'll be relatively safe using our real last name when the time comes, but for now it takes a minute to remember to say *Gabriela* instead of *Josephine.*

He stares at my hand and doesn't bother shaking it. I awkwardly drop it and keep talking.

"I will pay for this. I swear it." I stare at the dent in his car, which is an impressive sports car of some sort. I don't know cars, but it's even nicer than my newly leased Lexus. "Here, let me get my insurance information…I mean, you know where I live too, so you can always hunt me down if you don't trust me."

I chuckle and it dies in my throat when he doesn't respond.

"Okay. Maybe I'll just give you my number. Hang on a sec, I'll write it down." I grab a receipt sitting in my cup holder and write my number on it. "Again, I'm so sorry."

He takes it but doesn't acknowledge it, just stares at me with those eyes that seem to see inside my soul. He doesn't like what he sees. That much is obvious when he tosses my card in his bag and leans down until he's an inch from my face.

"You talk too much," he says, his deep, raspy voice dripping over my skin like hot lava. I shiver and he notices, the ice in his eyes crisping into frosty ice cubes. "This little incident and the one earlier will cost you, but I'm sure I can come up with a few ways for you to repay me." His eyes flicker to my lips and that whole lack of air becomes a problem again. He leans back and crosses his arms, and I feel dismissed.

His glare is an assault on my nerves and I back away, needing to put distance between us. I have a feeling this guy isn't going to make anything easy for me. Too hot for his own good, and entitled bastard is written all over him…yet my heart is quadrupling over itself.

I hustle into school and barely catch my breath when I reach my locker. One positive thing about the altercation with *hot neighbor guy* is I didn't even notice all the kids staring at me on my way inside. I take my blazer off and hang it in the locker, grabbing the notebooks I'll need for the next couple of classes. When I slam it shut and turn around, it's like all of us turn as one to appreciate the guys walking in the door. The hot bastard—his name is a work in progress until I find out what it is—is flanked by two other hot guys. The one on his left is pale with black hair that you just want to sink your hands into and explore. The one on the right has dark skin, a captivating smile, and his body is chiseled stone. They're both beautiful, but I'm captured by the guy in the center. The way his hair slightly curls over his ears and his too-toned for high school body.

The second he sees me staring, I try to look away, but my gaze is drawn back to his. I wish I could control my curiosity, but it's impossible. Girls swarm them in a matter of seconds and still his glare seems to have it out for me. I remind myself he looked like that before I hit his car—that scowl was on his face earlier...when I almost hit him the first time. *Dammit.* But then one of the beautiful girls next to him says something and he looks down at her and smiles. My heart caves into itself. Nope, it's just me that he hates.

The next few seconds play out like a bad movie. The group shifts all of their attention on me and suddenly they're moving my way. I back into my locker, wishing I'd made a run for my class instead of standing here waiting.

He stops in front of me and they all check me out like I'm the lab specimen up for dissection.

"This is the new girl," Hot bastard says. "Allow me to introduce myself. I'm Raf Barron. Stay the fuck away from me and we'll be all right." He points at the dark-haired guy and backs up. "Henry, let's go."

"Hello, new girl." Henry has the slightest hint of a British accent. My eyes widen. I've always loved a delicious accent. "Ashton, you coming?"

Ashton smiles at me as he passes. He seems like the

nicest of the bunch, but who knows? I'm sure his asshole side will make an appearance.

I clear my throat. "I'm Gabriela. Nice to meet you guys."

Raf turns around, his brow furrowed in the middle, as if the sound of me talking grates on his last nerve. "Let's get one thing straight, you're nobody here. You keep your head straight and your mouth shut...don't speak unless you're spoken to...and maybe you'll survive Longlake. Have I made myself clear?"

"Wow, for someone so good-looking, you sure are a dick."

I shouldn't have said that out loud. But my biggest regret is acknowledging that I think he's good-looking. The dick part, he needed to hear loud and clear.

CHAPTER TWO

Raf's cheeks tinge with pink. Embarrassment? No, I doubt he knows the meaning of embarrassment. Rage? Yes. He stalks toward me in the next second and you could hear a pin drop around us. He has the attention of everyone in the hall and it's crowded because the bell is about to ring.

"What did you call me?" His voice is deadly calm.

My insides quiver and his eyes trail down my body like he can hear each flutter of my nerves. He gets caught on my chest for a few extra moments and it makes the butterflies flap even harder. Damn him and the way my body responds to him.

"You heard me." My voice is barely above a whisper, but I take a deep breath and stare up at him defiantly.

"Come on, Raf," Ashton says. "Let it go."

"Back off, Ash." Raf glances at Henry and the two of them chuckle. *Can you believe this girl?* I can only imagine the other things they're saying with their ESP, but I'm pretty sure I read that look loud and clear.

"I'll let it slide for now," Raf says, his face inching near mine again, "but try it again..." He knocks my books out of my hands and steps back when my notebooks slide across the floor. He lifts both hands up, attempting to appear innocent, but his smirk is too obnoxious to pull that off as he walks away.

I bend to gather all my things then sag against the locker. This could be harder than I expected. Senior year might be the longest one yet.

Henry is in my first hour and he seems less intimidating without Raf. Ashton is in my next two classes, and he smiles tentatively when he sees me. I appreciate him trying to help me out before with Raf even if it didn't change anything. He seems harmless enough, but I don't bother testing that theory. I stay out of his way.

I sit at a table by myself at lunch, keeping my eyes down and my attention focused on my food.

And what a lunch it is.

This is fancy dining at its best. I dig into the lasagna and my eyes roll back in my head. My mom doesn't let me have carbs when she's around, so this carbfest will be worth every calorie.

A tray clatters across from me, and I groan mid-mouthful, when Raf, Henry, and Ashton sit across from me.

"You having a foodgasm, Gabi?" Raf asks, elbows on the table as he watches me nervously swallow.

I wish he wouldn't insinuate the word *orgasm* to me in this setting. All mean and vicious instead of how exquisite an orgasm can be otherwise.

Instead of responding, I take another bite.

"I asked you a question." He leans forward and dumps

my tray of lasagna all over my white shirt. I stand up, gasping, looking down as the food drips onto the floor.

I'm momentarily stunned and then I jump into action, leaning across the table and pouring his drink all over his head.

He seems surprised for a second and then he grabs my wrist, holding it in place.

"We've got a fiery one, boys," he says. "She'll be fun to tame."

No one bothers to come to my defense this time, but I know everyone's eyes are on us. I look around and notice that a group of students have the attention of the few staff members in the room...not to help me out, but to provide the perfect distraction for Raf to get away with this.

Raf nods when I turn back around. "No one to save you here." He grins a panty-melting grin and I feel it all the way to my bones. They get up and walk away, Raf's swagger making me sick to my stomach.

I hurry to my locker, grabbing my blazer before my next class. I don't know what these guys are trying to prove, but they'll learn soon enough that I don't scare easily. Even when I'm shaking everywhere...

***

My mom is cheerful when I get home. I eye her suspiciously when she smiles at me and motions for me to take a piece of fruit out of the elaborate fruit basket sitting on the counter. One, I still can't get used to her being home so early, and two, she is rarely cheerful. Since *After,* she hasn't been cheerful.

"Help yourself. Isn't this beautiful? It came from the Cromwells. They live nearby. Mr. Cromwell is a well-known author and I met his wife at a charity function last week. It will help if we establish a friendship with them. They're coming over for dinner tonight. You'll need to be presentable at seven o'clock. Wear something nice, okay, Gabriela?"

So much for asking how my day went. I realize I never settled the car situation with Raf. Hopefully, I won't be grounded from using my car once he decides to collect.

"I have homework," I mumble, biting into an apple.

"So you'll get your homework done now, and be down here with your smiling face by seven. I'm not asking..."

If I could be paid for the times I've heard her say, "I'm not asking, I'm insisting..." I'd have no need to ever work in my life. I'd be independently wealthy and could retire on a sandy beach somewhere, drinking umbrella drinks.

I don't dare argue. I'm too tired to win and wouldn't even if I was well-rested. Sarah or "Sookie" Sinclair—either persona is a force who refuses to be disregarded.

The Cromwells arrive at seven on the dot and I reluctantly make my way down the stairs in my "presentable" attire. My hair swishes around my waist and elbows as I walk.

Turns out I'm the one surprised once again. The Cromwells have a son my age and turns out I know him. Ashton stares up at me and grins, and I almost stumble down the stairs. He's not as tall or as handsome as Raf, but he's not suffering in the looks department. Not at *all*.

His hair is buzzed, which draws all of my attention to his deep brown eyes and full lips.

"*Hello*," he says with a smirk.

I lower my eyes to the floor, uncertain if I have bullying

to look forward to in my own home or if we're going to perform the act of all acts. Pure fakery. "Hello."

My mom holds onto my elbow. She looks like a different person when she's out of her stage makeup and wearing conservative clothes...or clothes at all. Tonight, she's playing the part of Suzy the homemaker. "This is Stuart and Lisa Cromwell and their son, Ashton."

The Cromwells are a striking couple with a dignified air about them. They must not recognize my mother—I doubt they'd be here if they did. Mr. Cromwell holds out his hand and I shake it, then Mrs. Cromwell's, and last of all, Ashton's.

"And this is my daughter, Gabriela," Mom says. "Ashton goes to Longlake. He's a senior too," she adds.

It's hard not to do a full eye roll, but I hold it in. "Yeah, we've met."

"Oh." My mother shakes her head and grimaces when I don't say anything else. "Gabi has spent most of her schooling at home, so it's a new experience at Longlake, I'm afraid. I think you'll be great for her, Ashton."

My eyes widen and I shoot her a look. My lack of "experience" is because of her isolating me, but I don't say anything. Of course, she's studiously avoiding me. I feel the color rise on my cheeks and look at Ashton again. He's grinning wide, enjoying the show.

The dinner feels never ending, between the heat in Ashton's eyes as he watches me across the table and our parents getting to know one another. Ashton's parents brag about him being the star quarterback at school. Apparently, he already has several schools interested in giving him a full-ride scholarship. I couldn't care less about football, but I try to act interested. I do think it's cool that he could get a great scholarship doing something he loves. With everything that happened with Luke and the fallout afterward, I got so far offtrack with school that it will take a miracle for me to make up for it. It'd be nice not to worry about getting in somewhere.

When they leave, with my mom promising Ashton that I'll watch for him at school tomorrow, I collapse against the door and stare at her.

"What was that about?" I groan.

"What are you talking about?" Her voice is nonchalant, but she has to bite the side of her mouth to keep from smiling. "It can't hurt you to get to know Ashton," she says. "He seems like a sweet kid...you heard his parents—he's the star quarterback and will have his pick of schools. We're new to this town and you wanted to *experience life*." She does jazz hands and I groan. "He'll be a good friend to have, but you have to make a little more effort."

I'm too annoyed to speak. I go upstairs and slam my door.

Ashton was nice tonight. But I wonder what he'll be like tomorrow when Raf is watching.

"Your mom was okay with you coming out this late on a school night?" Laura sits across from me at a coffee shop near my house.

"She doesn't argue with me when I say I need to meet with my sponsor." I smile at Laura. She was recommended to me at my first Long Island AA meeting and I've been happy with her so far. I didn't love Patricia, my sponsor in Vegas, so that was no big loss. Laura is down-to-earth and much easier to talk to than Patricia, who was older than my mom and more judgmental.

"How's it going at school?"

I crinkle my nose and she copies my expression. "Uh-oh. Well, let's get to the big question. Has it made you want to drink?"

"No, not really. I feel pretty solid. I guess I just wanted to see you *before* I get that feeling because...this school will be a challenge."

A guy's face flashes across Laura's phone and she groans, picking it up to turn the sound off. "My brother," she says. "Forgot to turn my sound down. Sorry about that. I'll call him back later."

"I won't be long. We could've done this over the phone...I just needed to see one friendly, non-manipulative face today."

"Ouch, that bad, huh?"

"I don't know if I'm cut out for this, but fortunately, it's just the one year, right?"

"Right. Look, you're beautiful and nice...you're smart. It might take time, but I think you'll find your crew. You only need one true friend to make a difference. Join a few clubs, see if you can find your people." She smiles and takes a sip of her hot chocolate. "And call me if it gets to be too much."

I nod, looking down at the napkin that I can't stop picking apart. It's been a long time since I've been this stressed and not had a drink. "I know you're right. Thank you. This has helped."

"Every day is a new beginning."

"*There's* the mantra." I laugh and she gives me a fake scowl before laughing too.

I hope she's right. I already need a new beginning at Longlake.

CHAPTER THREE

The next morning, my mom is still home. Is she purposely trying to ruin my life? I'm not used to her not being a full-time porn star. I think some of her edge is due to her retirement...and the lack of orgasms she's "faking" these days. Do I sound bitter much?

I've already ignored a call from my dad today—he's three hours earlier than we are and sounded agitated to be leaving a message. I'm not ready to talk to him yet. The problem is I never will be. I hate that he even knows where we are.

I pour a cup of coffee and brush past her to take it upstairs while I get ready, when she stops me.

"I told Ashton's mom you could use a ride to school this morning."

I freeze. "Mom, seriously? That's so embarrassing. And so *obvious*," I let out a long groan. "Let me get to know the guy first before pushing me on him. We don't even know him. I thought you wanted me to have nothing to do with guys. Remember that?"

"I wanted you to have nothing to do with Luke. There's

a difference."

"What about us fitting in? This is desperate." I throw my head back, staring at the ceiling. "I'll drive myself."

"Give him a chance. I'm not asking, Gabriela, I'm *insisting*."

"*Mom*." I shake my head. When I'm upstairs, I set the coffee down and try to still my shaking hands. I'm too mad to think straight. Why do I let her get to me?

I leave without saying bye to her, something I'll hear about later, but I hope to get out of here before Ashton shows up. I don't want to make him mad, but I'm not comfortable riding with a guy I still don't know.

He pulls in just as I'm opening my car door. Damn.

His muscular body fits the whole sports car vibe and I reluctantly slide into the passenger seat. The smell of fresh soap and pine hits me when I close the door. He eyes me appreciatively and my nerves relax somewhat. If he wasn't always hanging around Raf, I'd think he was a nice guy.

"Looking good this morning, Gabriela." He buckles up and then leans his back against the door to look at me. "I can drive tomorrow too if you want."

"That's okay."

"I mean, I'm not gonna turn down a chance to hang out with you," he says.

Heat rushes up my neck and face and it gets hotter as he chuckles.

"So what are the people like at Longlake?" I ask as we pull out of the driveway. I don't see Raf, which is a relief.

"Most just want to have a good time, honestly," he says. "What was your first impression?"

"So far it seems like there are a lot of privileged brats." I shrug. "And bullies."

His groan is loud and I grin in spite of myself. His laugh is contagious and surprisingly sets me at ease.

"Sorry about Raf. He's...tortured."

"What do you mean?"

I glance at him and catch him staring at my chest. With a porn star mother, my boobs are nothing in comparison, considering hers are fake, but they're more than a handful. Still, most guys I've met never look me in the eye. He seems embarrassed when he sees that I noticed and I turn back to the road, ignoring my nerves. It would be nice to have someone interested in getting to know me. Maybe my mom is right—maybe Ashton can help.

"Just that he's not as bad as he seems, but he can also be a real asshole at times. Case in point, the lasagna."

"Oh, you think?" I shake my head. Unbelievable.

"I don't know why you seem to set him off."

"So it's *my* fault."

"No. That's not what I mean at all. I'm sorry for the way it's been so far for you at Longlake. It'll get better."

When we pull into the parking lot, speak of the jerk himself. Raf and Henry are leaning against Raf's car, arms folded and looking like a magazine layout. Raf's eyes narrow when he sees me in the car with Ashton.

"We have some of the same classes, so I'll see you later," I say before getting out of the car.

"Yeah. Hey, Gabriela? Watch your back, okay?"

I get a chill across my skin and nod. So many questions, but now is not the time or place. He steps in place next to me as we walk toward the school and I glance at Raf as we walk past. He looks ready to explode. I sigh.

"Your friends are waiting. Thanks for the ride." I give Ashton a little wave and he starts to say something but I rush off before he can.

Things get worse at lunch. I'd hoped my table partners would keep walking and not do a repeat of the day before, but I'm not so fortunate. Raf and Henry walk up and Henry says something under his breath that sounds like, "Sweet tits," but I can't be sure. Raf punches him in the arm and Henry's tray nearly goes flying. He gets a grip on it before we have another *lasagna down my shirt* situation. Raf sits next to me and when Ashton comes up a few minutes later and sits on the other side of me, Raf growls.

I look at him incredulously. "Did you just growl?" I spit out.

He snorts next to me and again I look at him like he's crazy. It's the most awkward lunch I've ever had and I'm actually relieved when four girls walk up and start talking to the guys. They're the girls I see falling all over themselves anytime Raf, Henry, and Ashton are nearby.

"Raf, you should have a party this weekend after the game since your dad's going out of town. We can have a bonfire by the water," Ashton says.

Raf is digging into his food like he's starving. "That can be arranged," he says and takes another huge bite of his cheeseburger.

"I'll be there." A tall redhead leans over Ashton so she can show him and Raf her cleavage.

Ashton clears his throat. "This is Amber." He points at the others one at a time. "Heidi, Melanie, Jen."

The table goes quiet.

I hold up my hand and don't bother smiling at any of them when they don't acknowledge me.

"Gabriela should come too." Ashton peers around me to Raf then grins at me.

"She isn't invited," Raf says, pushing away from the table.

Ashton frowns. "Raf, man. Don't be an asshole."

They both have balls, I'll give them that.

Raf's tense as he stands up. But when a slow smile flits across his lips, that scares me more than his typical scowl. "You know what? I don't think we can trust you to keep your mouth shut, can we, new girl? You're gonna run home to Mommy and tell her there's a party going on, aren't you?"

"It's Gabriela, remember?" I mutter under my breath. "And I won't say a word. I wouldn't go to your party even if I was invited."

I wonder what happens at his parties that he'd be concerned about my mom finding out about it.

"We've already decided you're not good enough for us." Heidi's lip curls up with disgust. She's the one I've seen hanging on Raf the most. I wonder if they're a couple. "You're a charity project and we don't want to take you on." She laughs and her girlfriends all fall in line, laughing along with her.

I shrug. "I live in the same neighborhood as Raf, so I must not be too bad off."

Her head whips around to Raf. "Is that true?"

He rolls his eyes and grabs my arm. "Word with you."

I follow him into the hall after I take care of my tray. He's out there already and when I step out, he cages me in with his arms.

"Here's how we're going to do this. You owe me." He waits for me to respond, but I just fold my arms across my chest and wait for him to finish his nonsense.

It seems to throw him off when I don't say anything.

"You pay up and I'll let you come to my party."

"I said I'd take care of the car and I will. I don't need a pity invite to come to your stupid party."

He leans in closer and there it is—that swirly feeling in my gut again, damn him. He's so close, our lips could touch if he just leaned in a teensy bit closer. My heart gallops away and I feel like I'm going to hyperventilate. I want him to kiss me more than anything. *No, don't be an idiot,* I reason with myself. But my body isn't paying any attention to reasoning.

"You're my toy to bat around so you're coming to the party." The seduction in his voice doesn't match what's coming out of his mouth and I frown, wishing I knew what this guy's problem is. "Ashton wants in your pants, pure and simple. And you look at him like you wouldn't mind."

"He does not," I scoff but wonder if he's right. I have seen Ashton checking me out several times. "Why would you care who wants in my pants?"

"I'm trying to decide how I'm going to make you pay first...and he doesn't fit into my plans. Tell him you're not interested and I'll see you Friday night."

"There's no way I'd ever come to your party." I say it without thinking and then wish I could suck the words back in.

His face goes through a series of expressions that have me wanting to both console and slap him. It settles on thunderous and I take a step back but the wall won't give.

He leans by my car and I feel his lips brush against it, sending goose bumps scattering across my entire body. "Dare on," he whispers.

My face heats and I swallow hard. I just want to go to school in peace, make decent grades, maybe have a date or two here and there. Is that too much to ask?

Raf's arms drop and he walks away, gloating. I can't go

to that party, and I need to make sure my mother is as far from home as possible on Friday night so she doesn't call the cops if it's loud. I can't count on her to be as cool as I want her to be.

When Ashton walks into calculus, Raf turns to see if I'm paying attention. Two girls are flanking Ashton and he's smiling at both of them appreciatively. One of the girls leans in and whispers something in his ear. She hands him a piece of paper and he puts it in his pocket. Looks like both Raf and I misread Ashton's attention toward me, which, I have to say, is a relief. The last thing I want is come between friends and this rivalry with Raf doesn't seem like it will ease up any time soon.

But when Ashton sees me, his eyes light up. "Hey, there you are."

He lifts a hand up to the girls and I see their shoulders fall when he looks at me. The one who gave him the paper glares when he sits next to me. I avoid looking at Raf, but I can feel the tension radiating from the other side of the room.

"How's it going?"

"Everyone's been okay. I like most of my classes. The last one was boring, but the rest haven't been bad."

Mr. Johnson comes into class like he's on fire. Papers stick haphazardly out of his folders, and overall, he looks like he hasn't slept in a week. The guy needs a vacation. Or to get laid. Maybe both.

"We have a quiz today," he says and the class groans. "I know it's early, but it'll be fun, I swear."

He hands out the papers and drops one of his folders,

sending a slew of quizzes flying across the room. Several kids laugh out loud and when no one else moves to help him, I get up and gather his papers, handing him a tidier stack.

"Thank you, Miss Sinclair. You deserve extra credit for your kindness." He grins and pushes up his glasses, leaving them even more crooked.

"*Ass kisser,*" someone whispers loudly and the room cracks up.

I sit back down and there's a note on my desk. I pick it up and glance around to see who wrote it. Raf's scowl is even deeper, three deep grooves etched between his brows. I swallow hard and open the note.

It won't be long before everyone knows what a slut you are.

I look at Ashton and he glances up with a slight smile. Raf is staring at his book and the girls I met at lunch are behind me, either digging in a purse or straightening notebooks. The girl across from me looks over and I hold up the note.

"Did you see where this came from?" I whisper.

She shakes her head. "No."

I stick the note in my folder and focus on the teacher for the rest of the class. It's just someone trying to intimidate me. They couldn't know anything about me yet...and how would they ever find out about Luke?

CHAPTER FOUR

The next day in the bathroom, I overhear a few girls talking before I flush the toilet. It doesn't take long to know exactly who it is. I would recognize Heidi's baby girl voice anywhere. I imagine her swirling her fingers around her long blond hair. Her hands are constantly in her hair.

"I am missing Raf's cock so bad." She laughs and my mouth drops open.

I guess that answers my question about them being a couple.

A pang of jealousy rips through me and I try to shake it off. I'm *not* interested in Raf Barron. Not even close. Just *no*.

"I hate school. My parents haven't let me go out all week. I'm counting on the party Friday night to have a little catch-up session." Heidi giggles.

"You sure you two are still a thing? I thought you weren't around him all summer." I'm not sure which girl it is. Melanie and Amber sound alike. Oh, maybe it's the one who doesn't talk as much...Jen.

"We'll get back to normal now that we're back at

school." Heidi doesn't sound as sure of herself now and it makes me smile.

One of the others says something I don't quite catch about Henry and Ashton.

"I'm needing some diversity in my life," she says. "Henry is the hottest Milaysian I've ever seen."

I roll my eyes so hard they hurt.

"I'll take Ashton. I can't wait for the game Friday. He is so hot when he plays." Pretty sure that was Jen.

"You'll have to fight Becca and Heather for him. Becca gave him her number."

I try to peek through the little crack through the door but I can't see anything. *Come on, hurry up.* I'm antsy waiting in my stall for them to leave before I go out.

I hear something rustling and then the smell of weed fills the bathroom. I stare up at the ceiling. Great. If I come home smelling like weed, my mom will throw a fit.

"Want some of this?" Heidi asks.

"Nah, I'm good with the pot."

"This is way better, I swear."

I try again to see what they're doing out there.

"What do you guys think of the new girl?"

"Skank." Heidi laughs and grabs a paper towel. "I don't know why the guys are all about her boobs and ass. It's not like either are even all that big and she's not even as tall as you or me, Melanie." Their footsteps fade and when they walk out of the bathroom, I loosen up. I spritz body spray in the air and walk into it, hoping it wipes out the smell.

I'm not too bothered by them. Raf is harder to handle than the girls are. I'm more used to girls being mean than a hot guy who's mean to me for no reason. In my old neighborhood in Vegas, the mean girls were plentiful.

You did put a dent in his car, I remind myself. But no, it feels more personal than that. I look around before I step all the way out of the stall and wash my hands, hurrying through the soap so I don't miss the bell.

Lunch is even more of a disaster than the day before. Girls swarm our table. I can't figure out why Raf insists on sitting by me when he dislikes me so much, but it's become a thing. I'm ignored by the girls, except for little snubs here and there. Nothing too over the top. Jen tries to sit between Ashton and me and I stand up and walk away. I'm not in the mood to compete over a guy.

I'm surprised when Ashton follows me out.

"Did I do something wrong?"

"What? No, you didn't," I tell him, reaching in my bag for a piece of gum. I offer him a piece and we walk to our lockers. "Your friends don't like me. Hey, what did you mean when you told me to watch my back?"

"Just that we're not the most welcoming group at Longlake."

I snort. "You think?"

He grins.

"You're not so bad."

He shrugs. "I'm not much better."

"Why are you being nice to me? You seemed like you could go either way that first day..."

"Your mom has been nice to my mom and she...needs more friends. It's hard being black in this neighborhood." He shuts his locker and looks away. "I do all right. Playing football helps. I watch out for Jen, make sure those girls treat her right. Only one other black kid here—freshman dude, Josiah." He chuckles but rolls his eyes. "Not as easy for my mom, so I was grateful when your mom reached out, had us over." He pauses and turns to face me. "I'll work on Raf, okay? He's not that bad."

"You know what? It's okay. I get that everyone has known everyone forever. Don't worry about me. I just want to get through this year...I don't need a bunch of friends." I wave my hand and shake my head.

One or two friends would be nice...

I keep that to myself.

I slam my locker door and jump when I realize Ashton has moved next to me. He leans against the locker next to mine.

"I think he's into you."

Something slams across from us and I turn around. Raf's watching us, arms folded.

"This is cozy." He's staring at Ashton like he wants to pummel him into the floor, but Ashton just grins.

A guy walks by and when he sees Ashton and Raf, he reaches out and they all bump fists.

"Have you met Toby yet?" Ashton asks.

I shake my head, although the guy does look vaguely familiar. I can't figure out where I would've seen him. He checks me out. Ugh. Guys are so predictable. In Toby's defense, he moves on a lot quicker than most of the other guys here have.

"Hey."

Toby nods.

"I've gotta get to class."

"Playing hard to get," Raf says, sticking a thumb in each pocket.

"I'm not playing anything," I call over my shoulder.

"Maybe not yet." His voice is closer than I expect and raspy. "But when you do decide to play, it'll be with me."

I don't even bother guessing what he means by that. But why am I excited by the idea of it?

The girl that sits across from me in Mr. Johnson's class is already there when I arrive.

"Hey, I should've introduced myself already. I'm Luci."

I smile, grateful for what seems like a normal interaction. Everyone else has been so weird. I'm either invisible or I bring out the hostility when I walk in the room. I don't get it.

"I'm Gabriela."

"I know." She smiles back. "You've created quite the whiplash around here."

"What do you mean?"

"The most popular guys sit by you at lunch and the most popular girls already hate you." She holds up both hands. "Whiplash."

I frown. "Yeah, not what I set out to do. Where do you fall in all of this?"

"I'm smart." She laughs when I stare at her blankly. "Meaning I don't get caught up in all that shit."

I smile then. "I'm glad to know there's at least one normal person here."

"Don't get your hopes up," Raf says, dropping his books on the desk in front of me.

"You worry about you, I'll worry about me," I say. "I wish I knew what your problem was…"

"According to you, no one here is normal…except for Luci, so…there's your excuse."

Luci watches the conversation with her mouth wide

open, her gaze ping-ponging back and forth between Raf and me.

"You coming to my party, Luci? Friday after the game?"

Her mouth clamps shut and she swallows hard. "I didn't realize you knew my name. Uh—"

"I'll see you there," he says, laughing.

"Creep," I whisper.

I know he hears me by the way his jaw ticks and I feel a tiny rush of satisfaction. It helps take away the sting of him wanting everyone *but* me at his party.

CHAPTER FIVE

I wake up with the worst headache the next morning. My mom had a charity breakfast to go to and I text her asking about meds, but I don't hear back. By the time I leave the house, I've ransacked the cabinets and haven't found anything. I'm running late and my head is *screaming*. I should've just bought something on the way and dealt with the late slip.

I get out and slam my car door, taking a long swig from my water bottle. I stumble when I step inside the school and am a bit unsteady when I bump into someone in the hall.

"*Shit.*"

"You just can't stay away, can you?" Raf holds onto my upper arms with both hands and I feel like I'm spinning.

"*Oh.*" I clamp a hand over my head.

His forehead creases together in the middle and he looks at me in confusion. "Gabi, are you *drunk?*" he whispers.

"No. Don't be stupid," I groan and close my eyes in agony. "Migraine," I whisper.

"Come with me." He grabs my arm and drags me

through the hall and to the theater. A few students are leaving and look at us with curiosity. He texts something and then grabs me again, rushing me out the side door of the theater.

"Slow down. I'm gonna be sick."

"Almost there. This way." We go through the hall and to the back exit, slipping outside.

The air is brisk, like fall is deciding to skip ahead to winter, and he puts his arm around me, holding me against him. We walk behind the school and stop at the first of the sports fields. I push him away and throw up in the grass. I feel his hand on my back and motion for him to leave me alone. I hate being sick in front of anyone, but it's a next level of humiliating to be sick in front of someone who hates you. I stay bent over with my hands on my knees even after I've stopped throwing up, when Ashton and Henry pull up and Raf helps me into the car.

"You okay, Gabriela?" Ashton asks.

"Migraine," Raf says softly and no one else speaks as we drive. I try to will my stomach to stop turning and cover my eyes with both hands.

When we stop, Raf helps me step out of the car and I could swear his eyes soften as he glances at me, but he presses his lips firmly together in the next second and looks his normal growly self.

"Anyone home at your place?" he asks.

"No."

He changes direction and holds onto me as we walk down the driveway and then go through his gate.

"I should just go home. Please. I'll be fine."

"Come to my house. At least until your mom is home."

"You're almost being nice," I whisper.

"Shut it," he says under his breath.

We go in the front door and I lean sluggishly on the banister, looking around.

"Pretty. Everything's spinning though."

"Come here." He swoops me up in his arms and carries me up the stairs. I close my eyes and inhale his neck. He smells like soap and leather and cinnamon.

It smells like him in his bed too. When he tucks me in, lifting the blanket up to my neck, my stomach settles. He walks away and comes back with a bottle of pain meds, water, and a cold washcloth.

"Here, take this." He opens the bottle of medicine and drops two pills into my hand.

I swallow them and lean back.

"My mom used to say the cold helped." He places the washcloth on my forehead.

"Thank you, Raf."

He doesn't say anything. I stare at him for a long time, wishing I could figure him out, until the meds kick in. And then I close my eyes and drift off to sleep.

In my dreams, I hear the sound of a guitar playing off and on. It lures me in and out of consciousness and is the most beautiful sound I've ever heard.

I wake up with a start when Raf jumps out of bed. I didn't even realize he'd fallen asleep next to me.

"It's my dad," he whispers. "Shit. I don't know what he's doing here."

I sit up and the headache is still there but nothing like it was.

"How are you feeling?"

"Better. It's bearable now. I'll sneak out and go home.

Don't worry. Your dad won't know I'm here. Okay?" I bend down to grab my shoes and wince as the pain slices through my skull.

"You don't need to leave. Just hang tight. I'll see why he's home so early."

"No, really. Thanks for the bed." I finish putting on my shoes and slowly stand. Yay for non-spinning rooms. I pause when I see a guitar leaning against his desk. "Were you playing that earlier?"

He doesn't say anything for a moment and when he speaks, it's quieter. "Yeah."

"It was beautiful."

"Thank you. Just a little hobby. Not something my dad will ever be okay with me pursuing."

"I didn't realize. Would you want to pursue it, if he wasn't against it?"

"It's everything."

Something about the way he says that breaks my heart. "I'd love to hear more of your music. I'm sorry for pulling you out of school. I hope you don't get in trouble for it."

His eyes widen. "That's why he's home early. *Fuck.* I fell asleep—I forgot to remind Henry to fix our absences."

"Fix our absences? What are you talking about?"

"It's nothing. No big deal."

"Uh, yeah, it is. Don't let him get caught doing that or he'll get kicked out—"

His look pins me to the wall. "Why? Can't keep your mouth shut?"

"I'm *great* at keeping my mouth shut." I scowl back. "I was just trying to be nice. Don't get caught."

He's smug as he opens his window and motions for me to climb out. "I'm too smart to get caught."

I shake my head and put my legs over the window,

latching onto the tree. "Then why did you look so terrified when you realized Daddy is home? And you're seriously making me climb out a window..."

"Shut it," he mutters behind me.

I crawl down and glance both directions before running home. I take a chance and go out the back gate, ending up on the beach. Their view is as breathtaking as ours and I lean against the gate enjoying the waves and trying to catch my breath before making my way to our backyard. I step inside and am relieved when my mom still isn't home.

I check my phone and see a missed call from her and several texts from Ashton asking if I'm okay. I look online to see what assignments I missed and start on my homework.

I brace myself when I hear the garage door opener. My mom doesn't waste any time. I can tell by her face that she's not happy with me. I sit up taller when she comes into my room, shutting the door behind her.

"I was alerted that you left school today. Care to explain?"

"Did you not get my text about meds? I had a migraine and got a ride home. I'm sorry I didn't clear it first. I threw up at school."

She studies my face to see if I'm telling the truth. "You do look pale. Next time, do it the right away. We can't afford to draw attention, Josephine. If they think I allow my daughter to skip school, they'll be breathing down my neck. I thought this is why we moved across the country...so there was less of a chance that everyone would know about your past and mine."

"If you could just call the school and let them know what happened, I think it will be okay. I'll make sure not to do it that way again. Sorry." When her expression is still one of distrust, I add, "Hey, guess what? Ashton Cromwell asked me to his game on Friday night and to go out afterward. Is it okay with you if I go?"

What's a few little lies to make her happy? It's not exactly a date with Ashton, but I think it could be if I wanted it to be...if I wasn't afraid of how angry it would make Raf if I showed up at his party with Ashton.

I think of how sweet Raf was this afternoon and decide I'll go if my mom says it's okay. He doesn't need to dare me. I want to go.

And if I get too uncomfortable, I know how to sneak out of his window. I cover my grin with my hand.

Sarah Sinclair does not excite easily, but she squeals with this news. "I knew the two of you would be perfect together. Yes, of course, it's okay with me. You take after me with your way of luring a man in." She mimics pulling something closer. I cringe, the notion that I take after her in *anything* disturbing, but I nod. As long as I don't turn into her when I'm older. I stayed as far as I could from her pornos online, but I accidentally saw a clip of her when I was obsessively searching Luke's films.

Scarred for life.

She smiles at me and I give my head a little shake, trying to mentally erase that view of her mouth parted as she was impaled. I guess I should be glad it wasn't Luke doing the impaling, but yeah, there's no positive way to spin it. Some scars can never be erased.

I nervously smile back. It's strange to have a conversation go well with my mom since Luke...I mean *Before*. It feels upside down to make her happy.

"I tell you what. You do look pale. How about you lay low tonight, stay home tomorrow and rest, and then by Friday, you should be as good as new. I'll take care of all of it with the school, don't worry."

My mouth drops open a little, shocked at how she's bustling around like a new woman. Who knew agreeing to a fake date with Ashton would make my mother pleasant?

I pull out my journal. As I start to write about Raf, my pen pauses and I leave a sentence hanging. The last time I wrote about him was the day we met. Every time I try to fill in what's happened since, I can't. It's too humiliating. Too confusing.

Some things are better left unwritten.

And not wanting to tempt fate after having a decent day with him, I close my journal with a snap. I watch movies in bed, while my mom orders takeout soup. It's the best night I've had in a long time and so is the next day when I skip school and catch up on all the sleep I've been missing lately.

CHAPTER SIX

I get to school early on Friday and go to the library to return a book. When I reach my locker, Raf is waiting for me.

His eyes are that startling light blue today. Unsettling and beautiful; it's hard not to get hypnotized in them...especially when he looks as mouth-watering as he does this morning.

"You feeling better?" he asks, checking me out.

I open my locker and avoid looking at him any longer. I need to keep him at a distance. One day of sweet behavior doesn't undo the way he's treated me. "I'm fine. It's almost like you were worried about me or something. I was just having an off day."

"Do you get migraines a lot?"

I shrug. "Not too bad. Just depends on the stress—" I stop there. Raf isn't my friend. I don't need to start opening up to him.

"Listen," he runs his fingers through his hair and I'm not used to seeing him so nervous, "as much as I dislike everything about you, I don't like to see anyone in pain...that I'm not inflicting." He smirks, stepping closer to me. He puts his hand around my neck giving it a slight squeeze. "Can't afford to have you sick before the party tonight. Your mouth and my cock—"

"I won't be at the party."

If he could see inside my brain, he'd think I'm playing games with him, but it's just that he changes my mind about how I feel about him every other second. I was *this* close to caving, until he had to open his jerk mouth.

His face is thunderous as he leans closer to my face. "You'll be there or we'll have a big problem."

"Guess we're going to have a big problem then." I duck under his arm and skirt past him, grinning. It's nice to get the last word with him for once.

The day drags on forever. Ashton is waiting for me at my locker before the last class, smiling shyly.

"What's up?" I grab my things out of my locker and slam it shut. "You have a determined but nervous look on your face."

He presses his lips together, trying not to laugh. "Okay, that's some spot-on face reading." He sighs and I wait for him to spit it out.

"Come to the game and the party tonight."

"I don't think that's a good idea."

"I'll make sure nothing goes wrong. I swear. And you need to get to know everyone. It'll be fun, I promise."

"I don't know how you can promise that." I back up and lift my hand when he starts to say more. "Have a great game tonight."

"Just think about it," he calls out as I take off for class.

"What are you wearing on your date tonight?"

And this is why I should never lie to my mother. I look at her for a moment and say the quickest thing that comes to mind.

"Just jeans and a cute top. I'll be leaving soon."

I don't know where I'm going, but I will *not* be going to the game or the party. I'd hoped to drown my sadness in a long bath but forgot I'd lied to my mom about a date with Ashton. *Dammit.*

I go through the motions of touching up my makeup and kiss her on the cheek when I leave. She looks so excited for me, I feel like an even worse daughter than before.

I stop by a gardening store and lust after the plants for a long time before ending up at a cute bookstore. I devour several chapters of the new Sarah J. Maas book and sip a hot chocolate until they announce that they're closing.

When I'm walking to my car, I hear the chirp of another car and jump, but I don't see anyone. I get a strange feeling, the hair on the back of my neck rising. I chalk it up to the lack of enough lights in the parking lot but hurry to my car and get out of there. It makes me miss my favorite spots in Vegas. I knew which places to avoid and which were safe to be alone. It'll take time to fully be comfortable here.

For this time of night, my street is hopping. There are cars lined down the street and through Raf's gate, I can see his long driveway is full. The party must be in full swing. I pull into my driveway and am surprised that the music isn't blaring. A responsible party-thrower. For some reason, that surprises me about Raf. Too bad my mom won't have a chance to get mad enough to call the cops on the rowdy neighbors.

Mom is waiting up when I walk inside and I grit my teeth and smile, aiming for excited exhaustion in my expression.

"So...how was it?"

"Great!"

She smiles and then it falters when I don't say anything else. "That's it? Did they win?"

Oh shit. "Uh, yeah! So great. And the party was a lot of fun too."

She nods and then her eyes twinkle as she leans in. "Did he kiss you goodnight?"

I groan. "Mom. No. He didn't, okay? We're friends."

She lifts an eyebrow and looks me over. "Boys will never want to *just* be friends with you. Trust me. You probably intimidate him."

I cringe and shake my head. "Not true."

I walk past her and hear her behind me. "Well, that's not an all bad thing, I just mean—"

"Night, Mom. I'm tired."

"Oh, okay. Goodnight, Josephine."

I sleep in the next morning and when I wake up I scroll through Instagram. I've looked for Raf online before and there hasn't been much. He seems to avoid having his picture taken. But with a little snooping, I find gold. On Heidi Serrin's feed, there's a picture of Raf with his arms around her. I enlarge it and my eyes narrow on how cozy they are. She's laughing like she's the happiest girl in the world and I glare at the picture for minutes, hating him more the longer I look at it. The picture already has a few hundred likes. My stomach grumbles and I swallow hard, feeling a pang in my throat. I scroll down and see another photo and nearly throw up. It's a group shot of Henry next to Melanie Wethers, Ashton has Jen Ames in his lap, and Heidi's tongue is touching Raf's cheek.

Gross.

I see red.

My face and body feel like they're on fire and I toss my phone on the bed. I have no right to feel anything. I don't even like the guy. What right do I have to be angry at Raf? I even knew he'd most likely be with Heidi. I heard about her plans to reconnect—looks like she got her way. But knowing it and seeing it are two different things.

This guy is trouble. I need to stay as far away from him as possible. I can't afford to feel *anything* where he's concerned.

———

I've just had a shower and am starting a movie when I get a text from Ashton.

Ashton: Missed you last night. What are you doing?

Watching a movie.

Ashton: Can I come over?

I pause for a moment, not positive what he expects from me. I imagine Heidi's tongue on Raf and all the things I didn't see that most likely happened last night and start typing. I need to give Ashton a chance, at least as a friend.

Sure.

Ashton: :) See you in five.

I meet him at the door and we go upstairs to my room.

"How was the game?" I ask once my door is closed.

"We won."

I'm glad at least *that* lie was true.

"Congratulations." I forge ahead. "Looks like you had a successful night with Jen."

He grins and gets comfortable on the floor in front of the TV. "She's always aggressive after I win a game." He waves his hand. "Not interested. We're friends. What are we watching?"

"Oh. Why not?"

He glances back at me as I pick up a pillow and hold it up to my chest. "Why am I not interested?" He makes a face. "Just not feeling it." He shrugs. "Do I need a reason?"

I smile and point to the screen. "I'd started *It's Complicated*, but we can watch something else."

He laughs. "My mom loves this movie."

"I used to watch it with my grandma all the time. Missing her, I guess."

"Let's watch it."

We start the movie but don't get far before my mom knocks on the door. I jump and hop up, opening the door. Mom blinks when she sees Ashton is here.

"Oh, hello. I didn't realize we had company. Sorry to interrupt."

I'm so shocked by how calm she is about me having a boy in my room, I don't say anything. Ashton stands up and comes over to shake her hand.

"Hello, Mrs. Sinclair. I hope you don't mind—Gabriela and I were just watching a movie."

"Oh, please, call me Sarah. And of course I don't mind. You're always welcome."

He grins. "Thanks." He goes back to the floor and gets comfortable.

Mom's eyes widen at me and she bites her lower lip. It's

like we're two excited girlfriends all of a sudden. I return her crazy eyes, warning her to not be so obvious and she just grins and backs out of the room.

So weird, but I'll take it.

My phone starts going off and I ignore it. Ashton pauses the movie. "Do you need to check that?"

I shake my head. "Let me just turn off the sound."

I pick it up and see four missed texts from an unknown number. I gasp when I read the first message and look at Ashton to make sure that wasn't too loud. He's engrossed in the movie.

Since you completely disregarded my invitation, you'll have to pay.

I inhale a long, shaky breath and keep reading, my heart picking up with each text.

Tomorrow at 4.

My house.

You on your knees.

I put my hand on my head and ignore the image his words brings to mind. I look at my phone again and there's a new message.

Next time you ignore my request, you'll be on your knees for a week.

As angry as his texts make me, after Ashton leaves, I fall asleep thinking of the pictures of Raf with Heidi and how wrong it felt to see him with someone other than me.

CHAPTER SEVEN

I'm a bottle of nerves the next day. I take a shower and then a bath when I've sweated through two shirts. I put on makeup, which I don't usually bother with on a Sunday, but I need something to pass the time. Mom has backed off of lecturing me about how much makeup I wear to school, and in turn, I've toned it down a bit. I let my hair fall in loose waves instead of straightening it. When four o'clock rolls around, I'm still pacing the carpet in my bedroom. My heart is in my throat. I've lit candles, hoping that would calm me down, but nothing is helping. I keep finding new ways of spiraling down again.

I hear pounding on the door and I clutch my throat, shaking like a leaf. This is ridiculous. *He doesn't have an ounce of control beyond what I give him.* I say it out loud in front of my mirror the second time and give my T-shirt a tug as I walk down the stairs. My mom opens the door before I can stop her.

"Oh, hello," she says.

He smiles and it sends a jolt between my legs. I've never seen him so polite.

"Hello, I'm a friend of Gabi's."

"How nice to meet you. I'm Sarah," she says, holding out her hand.

He shakes it and then glances past her to see me standing at the bottom of the stairs. "Hi, Gabi."

I hold up a hand and can't find my words.

My mom turns to me with huge eyes and if I thought she was excited about Ashton, it's nothing compared to seeing Raf's hotness. Her mouth drops open and she mouths, "*Wow.*"

"I wasn't expecting you," I manage to say.

"Oh? We had a plan for 4, right?" He studies his watch and grins, all charm.

Oh, he's good. He's really good.

"Did you forget a date, *Gabi?*" my mom asks.

I narrow my eyes at both of them and point upstairs. "Let me grab my books."

Raf follows me up the stairs and my heart pounds harder with each step. When we reach my room, I close the door, my hands perched on my hips. Before I can say anything, his hands rest on the door on either side of my face.

"My mom is gonna think it's weird that you followed me up here," I whisper. She probably won't mind at all, but he doesn't need to know that.

"You have two seconds to walk across the yard to my house or we're doing this here." His demeanor is unruffled, completely calm and nonchalant. If his chest weren't rising and falling more rapidly than usual, I'd think he was completely unfazed by all of this.

"I don't understand. What are you *doing?*"

"Here or my place?"

I grab a book so my mom will be appeased and glare at him.

He opens the door and motions for me to step out. We walk downstairs.

"Walking to the library," I tell her.

"Okay, sweetheart. Have fun. Nice to meet you—you know, I don't think I heard your name."

But he either doesn't hear her or is in too much of a hurry because he's already walking out the front door. "Nice to meet you too, Mrs. Sinclair."

Neither of us bother to tell him it's no longer Missus.

I walk outside behind him and he takes my hand. The contact burns through me, a spark making contact for the first time. It feels like we're in a dream when we walk down each long driveway and then upstairs to his bedroom. He shuts the door behind him and leans against it, folding his arms.

The next thing I know, he has me pinned against the door, leaning down so his lips are an inch from mine.

"Are you ready?"

"For what?"

"You've eye-fucked me for long enough. It's time you deliver."

His words should repel me, but he's right. I've stared at him like he's an open candy box and I can't wait to eat my fill.

"What are you—"

His mouth is on mine before I can finish, but I inhale him in and we devour each other. The kisses I've experienced before were nothing like this. Not even close. And I can't believe it's Raf. I've wondered what it would be like, but I didn't think it would actually happen. His tongue flicks across mine and I whimper. He puts his hands on my ass and lifts me up so he doesn't have to bend so far down to reach me. And I lose all desire to put a stop to this.

I am drunk on him.

He grinds into me and kisses me so hard, I'm sure there will be bruises tomorrow.

Every single one will be worth it.

He wraps my legs around him and carries me to the bed, sitting down so I'm straddling him. He pulls back and brushes my hair off of my face.

"What's so bad about this?" he asks.

"Not a thing."

His tongue lines the shell of my ear and I shiver.

"Kiss me." He makes me lose my mind again with his tongue. His soft, full lips work their magic.

I don't know how I'll ever keep my hands off of him now that I know he can kiss like this.

This is his *destruction*.

He knows the torment he's capable of inflicting on me now.

I shouldn't let him know how much I like everything he's doing, but it's impossible to stop.

His hard length presses against me and he moves me so we're lined up perfectly. It feels so good I can hardly think straight. I arch against him and he groans. The feeling is such a power trip, I know I will be craving this from now on. When I grind into him again, he arches up to meet me. His hands go to my hips and he sets the rhythm, moving me up and down. I get lost in him, in his soft groans, the way his hands set me on fire. I've never felt anything like this. It's all too much, too much sensation, too many things I've never felt by anyone other than myself, and it doesn't take long before I shudder against him, crying out as I fall apart.

He inhales my sounds with his mouth and every inch of

my skin feels alive. Just then, a horn honks outside and he pulls away, and the moment is lost.

He moves me off of his lap and I hurry to straighten my clothes, the heat rushing to my face with embarrassment of how I let myself go in front of him.

"You have to go," he says. "*Now.*"

"Oh. Okay." I put my hand to my cheek and turn around, so scattered I don't know if I should go out the door or out the window.

He shoves me toward the window. I guess that answers that.

I crawl out and latch onto the tree, looking down before I risk jumping. Toby Matthison is walking toward the front door and in the next second, the doorbell rings. Why would Raf care if we saw each other? Once I'm close enough, I leap to the ground and run to my backyard without another glance.

My humiliation is complete.

What was that even about? I guess it could've been worse. I'm surprised Raf bothered to make me feel good and then threw me out before I could return the favor, but the shame is right up there with the time I got caught making out with a guy named Louie at a homeschool co-op. A parent caught us and she told my mother within the hour. I was grounded for three months and after the day we got in trouble, he never spoke to me again.

Not to mention what created the *After*. I can't stand to think about that time. It was definitely worse than this, but it's way too close for comfort.

I wonder how Raf will treat me tomorrow.

I'm so confused right now, I don't know which end is up. I can't wait to get out of Longlake and move on to the next phase in my life, far, far away from here.

I dream of Raf, waking up several times in the night and falling asleep to his eyes spearing me and his cock creating friction in just the right place. I wake up more than once, breathless and shuddering as I whisper his name.

How has he managed to work his way in, when every day he gives me more reason to despise him?

It's a crazy sorcery he has over me and one I'm going to have to fight even harder from now on.

I'm stronger than this, *smarter* than this.

CHAPTER EIGHT

My mom is all smiles the next morning. I managed to avoid her when I came home from Raf's yesterday, but she has clearly not forgotten where we left off.

"Now I know why you were so nonchalant about Ashton," she says, her hands clasped together and eyelashes fluttering. "My god, that boy is *gorgeous*. I didn't know they made high school students like him." She picks up a pot holder and fans herself.

I wrinkle my nose and stick my head in the refrigerator. I let the coolness calm my heated skin and pull out a yogurt.

"Gotta run, Mom. See you later."

She sighs. "Okay, but I want the details of this new development later."

"It's nothing."

"Pfffft. That boy is *not* nothing."

I groan and she looks hurt. I know she's trying to get me to open up to her again, hoping we'll be close like we used to be, but I'm a different person now. We're both different.

"I'll talk to you later, Mom. Promise." I kiss her cheek and it seems to satisfy her.

"Josephine?"

I turn back and my mom's jittery, her leg shaking hard enough to make her bracelets rattle. "Yeah?"

"I have a date tonight."

"Oh." *Oh.* I didn't expect that to hit me hard, but it does. "Okay."

"Are you sure?"

"Well, I don't get a say in your dating life, do I?" I try to smile, but it doesn't quite deliver. "I hope you have fun, Mom. I've gotta go."

She presses her lips together and nods.

I step outside. Ashton offered to drive me today and I didn't overthink it, I just said yes. On the front step is a bundle and I pick it up, moving the paper back to get a better look. I drop the flowers, looking around to see if anyone is out here.

Red lilies.

Shit. This day just keeps getting better.

Luke used to have a red lily waiting for me every time I went to his house. Every time we slept together.

I start shaking. It can't be Luke. There's a restraining order out on him and the last I knew, he had moved on with the playmate of the month.

Someone's playing a trick on me, but who?

Ashton pulls in then and I put the lilies in the garbage can outside before I slide into the passenger seat. I attempt to grin at him, trying to let my anxiety go and the guilt over yesterday with Raf. I don't know why—Ashton hasn't made any moves and I honestly don't know if he's interested or not.

When we get to school and step out of the car, he comes around to my side and waits until I've got my backpack on my shoulder before taking my hand. I lift an eyebrow at him, surprised that he's going there. I guess he *is* interested.

"What...are you doing?"

"Just go with it."

The guys are in the parking lot. Raf's eyes fall to my hand linked with Ashton and he turns away, muttering under his breath. The hate swirls around in his eyes and I can't figure out why he has it out for me.

You're not doing anything wrong, I remind myself. But I'm confused by the guilt swarming in my chest. Kissing Raf...what if he would've been different today after our kiss? Nicer?

I remind myself of the way he threw me out of his room afterward and sigh. I'm pretty sure that whatever I do will be the *wrong* thing.

I stop at my locker and Ashton leans in behind me, nuzzling my neck. I freeze and then he whispers, "Raf needs to learn a lesson."

"Is that a good idea?"

I can practically feel Raf's eyes drilling through me. Why I'm considering him, I have no idea.

Despite what he thinks, he *does not* own me.

"Do you trust me?" Ashton asks.

"I think so."

Ashton laughs and steps away. I'm so confused. I put my things away and grab the next two notebooks I'll need, slamming my locker shut. Ashton takes another step back and I bite my lip, reluctantly smiling at him.

I sit at a different table at lunch and when Ashton walks up a few minutes later, Raf scowls. He was already shooting daggers at me from our normal table. *What the fuck is his problem?*

He stands up and grabs his tray, stalking off. I'm tempted to follow him out, but I don't.

In the afternoon, the tension is up to security level during my class with Raf.

"Are you that desperate to forget our kiss? Now you're going to date that asswipe?" Raf whispers in my ear.

I shiver and turn to look at him. He's so close, our foreheads touch.

"I feel like a broken record. *You're* the asswipe." I try to lean back, but he closes in the distance. "And Ashton is your *friend.*"

"Doesn't mean he's not an asswipe. You're not into him."

"I don't have to answer to you about anything I do. And you're taken anyway—looks like you had a fantastic time with Heidi over the weekend."

His eyes spark and I see his lips twitch.

"You stalking me now, Gabi?"

The way he says my name sends liquid heat flooding through my veins.

"Simply stating the fact that you're occupied with someone and so am I. I've 'paid up' and now we're even. I don't know why we keep having this conversation."

"You're nowhere near paid up. We have an agreement and I don't want anyone else touching you. You weren't having any trouble getting off on me yesterday. Ashton not able to do it for you?"

My mouth drops open and I turn away from him, my

face hot. The teacher walks into class then and the conversation is over. I need to talk to Ashton. I'm not up for a game when I don't even know what we're playing.

As soon as the bell rings, I practically sprint out the door and I do whatever I can to avoid running into Raf for the rest of the afternoon.

I don't mean anything to him. He just wants to exert control. It's humiliating and I refuse to let him win.

When I get home, my phone pings.

Raf: Party at my place at 8. Be there.

I put a dress on and touch up my makeup. I don't bother responding to Raf's text and I don't even try to talk myself out of going. I want answers. I want to know what's going on between Raf and Ashton and I want to make this degrading behavior stop. I'm desperate to stop the crazy things Raf does to my heart, even when he's vile. I remember the way he leaned over me with the cold washcloth that day I had a migraine and the little voice in my head reminds me he is capable of being decent. Maybe even kind. I don't need to see any of the sweetness, it's better if I learn every loathsome thing there is to know about him.

My mom has already left for her date. I didn't ask anything about who she's seeing and she didn't offer any information. We were even more awkward than usual and I didn't need to make it worse by telling her I'd be at a party tonight. Although if she'd known it was at Raf's house, she probably would've gushed about how exciting it was.

I walk to Raf's at eight thirty, noting the fewer cars here this time. It's not a normal night for a party, which makes me wonder why he's doing this. And why do I need to be here? I think about the kiss in his room the last time I was here and my skin feels hot as I walk inside. The music is going and the living room is full of kids I recognize. Amber is dancing by herself, Melanie and Jen are dancing with Henry, and I look around for Heidi or Raf...but I don't see them or Ashton. Luci smiles at me as she dances with another guy from our class.

I feel hands tugging my waist backward. I yelp and try to turn but feel his mouth near my ear instead.

"You get all dressed up for me, Gabi?" Raf whispers.

"Why am I here?"

He moves us into a small, empty room and leaves the light off. I turn to face him and he nudges me backwards until I hit a washing machine.

"Laundry room, huh? Sexy."

"If I'd known you were looking for sexy, I would've taken you to my bedroom again. The laundry room was closer."

"For what?"

He lifts me up and sets me on top of the washer and runs his hands down the middle of my thighs, parting them and stepping between. I gasp and his mouth is there to catch it as his lips press into mine.

"Raf," I whisper.

"Gabi," he whispers back.

I pull away and he holds onto my head, winding his fingers through my hair.

"What are you doing?"

"I'm collecting your debt."

It's like a bucket of cold water is poured over my head and I push him away. I leap off of the washer and am almost to the door when he cages me in with his arms. His favorite position.

"No need to run. We both know you want me. Why are you fighting it?"

"Because you're a terrible person."

"Am I?"

I lean my forehead against the door and shiver when he moves my hair to the side and peppers my neck with soft, open-mouthed kisses.

"I don't understand why you're so mean and then kiss me like this. It doesn't make sense. I gave you my insurance information. Just collect the money already, let's be done with this nonsense."

"You think kissing me is nonsense?"

He turns me around and his tongue traces down the path between my breasts. He shifts from side to side and I gasp when his fingers reach up to tweak my nipples.

"Tell me you don't love every second of this torture, Gabi."

"I—" I moan when his palm covers my breast and he squeezes. He grinds into me and I cry out. And then he's on his knees and lifting my dress before I even know what's happening. "What—"

"If I touch you and you're not dripping wet, you can leave and I won't bother you again. Deal?"

I groan again, knowing what he'll find. He pushes my panties to the side and leisurely swipes his finger over my slick center.

"You're drenched," he whispers. "Just admit you're mine." He plunges a finger in me, in and out, in and out, and then two fingers, swirling my wetness around before thrusting back in. When he leans in and sucks my clit, I let out a long moan.

"Raf," I gasp.

I've been fucked by a porn star before, but it was

nowhere near as hot as this. Luke was always checking his angles. His room had mirrors everywhere, and he was so concerned about how he looked all the time, his attention always felt divided. At work, he spent most of his time on the foreplay, so when it came to the two of us in his bedroom, he was all about getting a quick fix. It took time before I realized he was all about his big finish and saved his partner's satisfaction for screentime.

Raf doesn't come up for air until I'm slamming my hands against the wall and chanting his name over and over again. I splinter apart into a thousand pieces and he takes his time, pulsing his fingers in as far as they'll go while my walls squeeze him impossibly tight.

He stands up and wipes his mouth and his chin and thrusts into me. "The next time I touch you, it'll be with my cock."

I shiver, the words feeling like both a threat and a promise. He pulls away and opens the door. The sliver of brightness from the other room casts light on his face. He smirks at me and I already know I'm going to hate what he says next.

"Go home, Gabi. Show's over."

CHAPTER NINE

I take my shame home, skirting past the couples making out in Raf's living room. No one pays much attention to me, which is a good thing. I'm sure I look even worse than I feel. Toby Matthison comes in as I'm leaving and he lifts his head in acknowledgment. I don't know why the guy makes me nervous, but he does.

I make it to my house and collapse against the door, feeling the weight of a thousand angsty nights. How do I manage to pick the worst guys to like? I wish I knew what Raf wants from me. He's given me two orgasms and I still haven't even touched him. It doesn't add up. Nothing about him does. I had one conversation with him, one day when he was kind to me. He opened up about his music, he took care of me. Where is that guy?

I think about the lilies that were outside the door this morning. I've been trying to put them out of my mind all day, but now that I'm home and it's dark and my mom still isn't home, I'm thinking about it a lot. I hope Luke isn't trying to enter the picture again. My dad will kill him if he finds out. *Literally*.

I take a long bath and try to read but fall asleep instead, startling when my mom walks into the room.

"Josephine?"

"What? What's wrong?" I sit up, panicked.

I glance at the clock and it's only ten thirty. It feels like midnight.

"There's been an accident with one of the students at Longlake. Do you know a guy named Toby Mathison at all?"

I rub my eyes and try to get my heart rate to return to normal. "You scared me to death. Not well, but yeah, I've met him. Why?" My stomach clenches and I lean against my headboard, thinking about the weirdness at Raf's house with Toby. "Is he okay?"

Her lips tighten and she backs into the hall. "It's not looking good. How well do you know—nevermind, we can talk later. I'm sorry I woke you. Go back to sleep."

I nod and she turns off the light. I lie in the dark staring at the ceiling for hours.

·

———

My mom is gone when I get up and I'm running so late I don't even have time for a shower. There's a text from Ashton asking if I need a ride and I tell him I'll drive myself.

I don't want to see Raf or Ashton today. I've had enough of the male species right now.

I wonder about Toby as I brush my teeth and wish I'd seen my mom again to find out if she knows anything else about what happened. I don't know much about him or his family.

There are police cars in the parking lot and everyone keeps their distance as they walk past the cars. There are two officers inside and I watch as they walk side by side to the office.

Raf, Henry, and Ashton are at their lockers when I reach mine and they're preoccupied. I make it to my locker without anyone acknowledging me. I hear their lockers slam one by one and Raf's arm brushes against mine as the three of them walk past me. *Real mature.* I lean into my locker and hear a girl giggle behind me. When I turn around it's actually two girls, Heidi and Melanie.

"*Burn,*" Heidi says, covering her mouth with her hand and laughing. "Looks like Ashton and Raf are already bored with you. It was a matter of time. You and your holier-than-thou attitude."

"You're talking to me? I hardly go around thinking I'm *holier* than anyone else. What does that even mean?"

Melanie's face crinkles into an ugly grimace. For someone so pretty, she can look really awful. Someone needs to tell her not to make that face.

Maybe I do have an attitude.

"Oh please, you have the biggest chip on your shoulder. Wonder why you're not making any friends—besides the ones you're trying to sleep with?" Melanie smirks and looks at Heidi for approval and seems to get it because she keeps going. "I think we satisfied them the other night. They've moved on. Raf for sure has, right, Heidi?" She gives her hair a toss and both of them turn around, walking away. They're like bookends, blond hair of the same color and length, with their designer jeans and matching boots.

I stand there for a few moments, wondering why I'm still on their radar after the weekend. The hall clears and I slam my locker shut, wishing I could walk out the door and start this day over, when a message comes across the intercom.

"Attention, all students, we will be meeting in the auditorium in ten minutes. Again, all students, make your way to the auditorium."

I almost put my books back in my locker, but instead, I go straight to the auditorium, barely managing to avoid getting trampled as everyone piles out of the classrooms. I bump into a hard body, stumbling back when I see that it's Ashton. He holds both hands up as he lets me pass.

"Sorry," he says, not looking me in the eye.

I don't know if he's mad I didn't ride with him this morning or if Raf has gotten to him. Who knows? I don't have time to figure it out.

As I round the corner and wait until the kids get through in front of me, I try to find a seat. One of the teachers tells us to find the first available seat and sit down. The first chair I spot is next to Raf and I hesitate.

"Gabriela, over here." Ashton waves, sitting a couple rows behind Raf. Color rises in Raf's cheeks as he stares through me.

My heart gallops away with me, and I sit next to Ashton feeling like I'm carrying a bag of bricks on my back. A hair flip catches my attention and I look down the row to see Heidi, Melanie, and Jen all staring at me.

What the hell is going on?

Ashton leans over and whispers in my ear. "You look beautiful today."

I smile at him gratefully, relieved to have at least one person being nice to me today.

Our principal, Mr. Saunders, walks to the podium and taps on the microphone. When he's satisfied that it's loud enough, he clears his throat and begins.

"It is with great sadness that I have to tell you about an accident involving one of our students here at Longlake."

The whispers of shock immediately spread throughout the assembly. Surely Toby's not dead?

Mr. Saunders holds his hand up and the talking ceases. "Toby Mathison was involved in a shooting last night and is in a coma. If anyone knows any details surrounding his accident, the police are asking for our full cooperation."

A gasp ripples through the gym and I try to see Raf's face, but I can't from where I'm sitting. I reach out and take Ashton's hand, looking at him to see his reaction. He stares straight ahead and squeezes my hand but seems to be in shock.

"We will have counselors on hand to talk to any of you who need help dealing with this traumatic state of events. There will be an ongoing investigation, and we ask that if you are asked to speak to a detective in the coming weeks, you do so, and then get back to your class as soon as possible, without talking amongst each other about the case."

Yeah, good luck with that. Doesn't he know this will be prime gossip around here? Longlake students are especially horrible about keeping secrets from each other. Someone like Toby, who's somewhat a mystery around here, is perfect material to hash and rehash. Heidi's head huddles next to Jen and Melanie as they act devastated about Toby. I wonder if they ever even hung out. In the next breath, I feel bad for having the thought. Maybe they were longtime friends—how would I know? Sometimes the lack of history I have with anyone at school is a blessing and a curse.

"Are you okay?" I ask Ashton.

"I just can't believe it," he whispers, still staring straight ahead.

I want to ask him so many questions, but he stands up suddenly and walks out of the auditorium. I watch as the door shuts behind him and wonder if I should go after him.

Raf also gets up and leaves and I stare after both of them, wondering what the hell is going on.

Throughout the day, everyone talks about Toby as if he was their best friend. Girls huddle together and cry, and several have to be excused each class to go talk to the counselors. I don't know if they ever even acknowledged him when he was here, but they sure want to be friends with him now.

This is such a harsh reminder that life can be ripped away in an instant. We can be walking around fine one day and hanging in the balance the next. It's too much to process.

Whether we admit it or not, I think most of us believe we're immortal.

My head is muddled as I walk back to my locker at the end of the day. I have a headache and trip over something right as I reach my locker, falling into it. I flip through my lock and open the locker, getting the shock of my life when a bucket of cold water drenches me. I sputter and wipe the hair out of my eyes. Kids around me start laughing and I look around, trying to see who appears guilty.

Heidi and Raf walk by and Raf's eyes widen as he looks me over. He lifts an eyebrow, smirking as he sees my face darken into rage. I turn back to my locker and scream, dodging backwards as a black snake slithers down from the top shelf. Raf laughs and steps around me, pulling the snake out with his bare hand. He walks to the door and frees it and turns expectantly toward me. Does he expect me to thank him? Or have a breakdown because of him?

I don't do either.

I'm trembling all over, but I get my backpack out, slam the door shut, and run out of the building before anything else can go wrong.

I sit in the parking lot for a long time before driving, trying to make sense of what's happening here. Was that Raf's work? Heidi's? *Why?* And what's going on with Toby?

I tried to call Laura last night, the need to talk to my sponsor greater than I remember it being in at least five months. It rings and rings, which isn't like Laura. And it's especially unusual for her not to return my call.

I've skipped my last class and sneak in through the back door when I realize too late that my mom is home. She's in the living room and I panic, wondering how I'll get past her. I start to back out the door when I hear a man's voice.

"He's out of jail."

"I didn't know he was *in* jail. You're supposed to keep me informed—why didn't I know about this? Where is he now?"

"I'm not sure where he is right now, which is why I'm here."

"You need to leave."

The talking gets quieter and when it sounds like they're walking near the door, I run up the stairs and shut my door. I sink my head into my hands and wish I could scream. Everyone is keeping secrets from me and I don't even know where to begin to try to unravel them.

My phone buzzes and I pick it up.

Raf: *I need to see you.*

I sigh. ***Why?***

Raf: *Meet me at the beach in back.*

I don't answer. Instead, I sneak out of the house and out the back gate. Raf is standing in the sand, barefoot, and staring out at the water. I watch him for a moment unde-tected before he turns and sees me.

"You need to leave Longlake." His whole demeanor is icy, and I rub my hands over my arms, feeling the chill near the water.

"Why?"

"Why do you ask so many questions? You don't belong there. You never should've come and now you *really* need to go."

"Does this have anything to do with Toby?"

He's next to me in the next second, his grip tight around my arm. "Don't even say his name."

"Why?" I whisper.

He puts his hand in his hair and tugs, looking around. I turn to see what he's looking at, but I don't see anything.

"Is someone following you?" I ask. "Are you in some kind of trouble?"

He leans his head back, his anger tumbling over the surface. "You've butted your nose into everything since you got here, and I'm telling you to stop. Leave. You're not welcome here, and you're not welcome at Longlake. It'll get a lot worse for you if you don't just go."

"I'm so confused. All I've tried to do is go to school and stay to myself. I've hardly even tried to hang out with Luci because I don't want her to be mistreated for being nice to me. You're making no sense." I push his chest away from me when he gets all up in my space. "Back off. I can't change schools. I don't want to move. Get over whatever ridiculous power trip this is and leave me the hell out of it."

"I wish I could. You're such a fucking inconvenience, trust me."

Ow. That hurts and I step back. "You don't seem to feel that way when your hand is between my legs."

He stalks forward, making me trip when I stumble back, until my back is against the fence and he's caging me in. His hand snakes down between my legs and he shifts my panties to the side, finding me soaked.

"You're such a whore. Just like your mother."

I rear back and slap him across the face, the sound a hard snap. It surprises both of us. He holds his hand to his cheek and I duck under his arms, running back to the house.

CHAPTER TEN

My head collides with a chest and I drop my purse. The contents scatter across the dirty floor and two girls glare at me when they have to step over makeup and extra pens. I barely slept at all last night after seeing Raf and I know it shows. Two hands steady me and I look up.

"We need to talk," Raf says.

"I have *nothing* to say to you."

"You look like shit." He pierces me with his crazy blue eyes and I feel like I'm sinking. I sag against him for a moment and then push him away.

"I wouldn't have thought you noticed. You despise the air I breathe." My voice breaks at the end. "Don't I always look like shit in your eyes?"

"Yes," he says with a smirk. "But you're wrecking yourself and I want to know why."

"What do you care? You want me to leave. Why can't we just agree to ignore each other?"

"We have unfinished business, Sinclair. Since you ignored what I said last night, it's your death wish."

"Why did you say that about my mother?" I stare him down and he looks everywhere but at me.

"You know the sayings about moms are always fighting words. I didn't expect you to go all slap happy on me." He chuckles and I want to slap him all over again.

I open my locker and ketchup sprays across my chest. He yanks me back and groans.

"I suppose this is your doing?" I yank my arm from his, not bothering to wipe off the ketchup.

"My stunts aren't this trivial."

Ashton walks up then and clears his throat.

"Are you still coming over to my house this afternoon?" Ashton asks. He and Raf fold their arms across their chests. They'd be drawing guns if this were an old Western.

"I was in the middle of a conversation with Gabi," Raf says, stepping closer to me.

"Well, we have plans," Ashton says, also stepping closer to me.

I'm trying to remember what I said to Ashton about his house. Everything is swimming together and I just need to go to bed. I'm in a tug-of-war and it won't end well for me. I won't be the winner.

"I'm just gonna go home today." I point at my shirt. "I need to change anyway."

A flash of something crosses Raf's eyes—he almost looks guilty for a second—but it's gone in the next second when Ashton puts his arm around my shoulder and hugs me close to him.

"My little klutz." He kisses my cheek and Raf's jaw ticks.

Raf backs away from me and turns around to walk away. I watch him go and when he turns around and points at me, my heart pounds with something hopeful.

"You wanna play?" He stalks closer to me and leans in my face, his lips a breath away from mine. "He's all yours. But don't say I didn't warn you...let's see what you're really made of."

The inspection he gives me when he backs up sends a chill through me. My mouth parts and I want to call after him, tell him not to go, to explain what he means, but my body is sluggish and in slow motion from the lack of sleep.

Ashton taps on the locker and snorts. "He's loving this." He tugs on my chin and turns me to face him, batting his sweet eyes. "Come over to my place?"

"You don't have to give me the puppy dog eyes to get me to do what you want." I groan.

He grins and stands up straight, his confidence back in full force. "Wasn't sure if you'd need convincing."

"Nope." My breath catches and my eyes well with tears. I remember my shirt with the ketchup smeared all over it and let Ashton lead me down the hall and to my car.

"Tomorrow I'll come over. I need to clean up." I get in my car and look up at him. He's still grinning even though I've turned him down and I'm glad one of us is in such a good mood.

"I thought you and Raf were friends? Why do you put up with him?"

He leans down and tweaks my nose. "We are." He bites the inside of his cheek. "This isn't him. I'm not sure what's going on with him right now, but you do bring out the worst in him."

I lift my eyebrows. "Then why do you keep pushing this?" I motion between the two of us.

"Couple reasons." He grins. "I'll see you tomorrow."

I wait, but he doesn't give me anything else. "Tomorrow."

I go home and take a shower, feeling more like myself when I get out. I relive the conversation with Raf a few dozen times and wonder what to expect from him next. I need to have another conversation with Ashton too.

I don't trust either one of them right now.

That thought is ringing in my ears even as I hear the doorbell. My mom won't be home for a while and I contemplate ignoring the door, but then the pounding starts.

I see Raf's car outside my bedroom window.

I run down the stairs and fling the door open, my heart racing. He stalks in, the fury still jumping off of him. He goes up the stairs and I hear him walk in my room before I realize he expects me to follow.

I'm annoyed but also curious, so I cave and head upstairs.

When I reach my room, he's pacing.

"So, you didn't go to his house." He stops and leans against my dresser, crossing his arms.

"I don't understand why you're being like this."

He walks up to me and runs his fingers down my cheek. "Have you slept with him yet?"

My heart trips over itself and I get on my tiptoes to get in his face. "What if I have?"

He turns around, walks to the window and slams his hand against the wall. My phone vibrates and Raf glances at it. When he sees who's calling, he slams his hand again and walks out of the room. I follow after him.

"Wait. Where are you going? What do you expect of me, Raf?"

He turns and stares at me before he leaves and for a

moment, all of his walls are down. Torment and despair and something like hatred. I shudder, rubbing a hand down my arm. He opens his mouth and I lean in, hoping whatever he says will reveal the truth.

Instead, he turns and walks out the door and I stand there watching him walk across the grass to his house.

Nothing neighborly about this relationship.

———

My interaction with Raf haunts me. Did he assume I was saying I'd slept with Ashton just because I didn't answer his question?

I think about drinking this away, I absolutely do. But I don't. I pace in front of the cabinet and even get a small knife to break the lock, but eventually put it away and go back to my room. I need to talk to Laura, but she still hasn't called me back. I could use a friend, or a distraction.

Something other than my sick fascination with Raf.

He thinks he owns me? A couple of orgasms and he thinks he can demand anything of me? *He thought that even before you kissed*, I remind myself. And he's most likely sleeping with Heidi.

I hope he isn't. God, I hope he isn't. But how can I have any thoughts about it when we aren't even together? I groan out loud and throw my phone across the room. It lands on the bed, so the result is anticlimactic but it helps distract me from hating Raf for two seconds.

By the time my homework is done and I'm in bed, my rage about Raf Barron is back with a vengeance.

I realize something before I fall asleep: I haven't thought of Ashton once since I left him in the school parking lot. If I wondered about there ever being anything but friendship between the two of us, I now know the answer to that.

It's like I'm in a different school when I walk down the hallways the next morning. The girls that have ignored me since day one are now looking at me with open contempt. A group of them parts and Raf, Henry, and Ashton stand in the middle of them. Heidi is hanging on Raf's arm and even though he doesn't acknowledge me, I can tell he knows I'm watching. He works too hard to not look my way. Henry glances at me and shakes his head, rolling his eyes and focusing his attention back on Melanie. Ashton is the only one who has a slightly guilty look on his face, but he sheds it quickly when I give him a tentative smile.

I've tried to avoid the bathroom as much as possible because I don't want to run into the mean girls and you never know when someone will be in here vaping, or worse. But I can't avoid it this time and sure enough, Amber is in the corner. I don't speak to her and she acts nervous to see me, quickly wiping white powder away from her nose. I do my business and get out of there, relieved that she's gone when I come out of the stall. I'm a little shocked Amber is doing this at school. She's not usually one of the girls I see high around here, but it seems to be more prevalent lately. Maybe everyone was on their best behavior at the beginning of the school year. Things are getting more comfortable now.

I exit quickly, hoping I don't find any new surprises in my locker. I open it standing as far back as I can, hoping to avoid whatever might come popping out. Nothing happens and I exhale a long sigh of relief.

I feel arms around my waist and jump. A broad chest circles my back and I glance over my shoulder. Ashton smiles down at me. I give him a shaky smile and gently push his hands off of my waist.

Lunch is painful. Luci had to go to a doctor's appointment, so I don't know where to sit. Ashton isn't in the lunchroom and the table I usually sit at is filled with my favorite crew. *Not.* I pull out a book and sit with my back to Raf. I don't want to see him, but I still feel his eyes drilling holes into me.

I need to focus on school anyway, I tell myself. I got a B on a quiz this morning, proof that my head isn't where it should be.

At this rate, it's going to be a tortuously slow school year.

I hear a commotion behind me and turn around when the chanting starts. I turn around and see Heidi doing something with her mouth while everyone around her chants: "Tie it! Tie it! Tie it!"

And then they start counting down the seconds.

She pulls something out of her mouth and holds it up triumphantly. I can't tell what it is, but she looks proud of herself and turns to Raf. My mouth drops when she wraps her arms around him, nuzzles her face into his neck, and he lets her.

My hands shake, my insides shake, I feel like a walking earthquake. I scoop up my books and throw my lunch away without finishing it. Ashton is walking in as I go out.

"Hey, you're leaving already?"

I keep walking and throw up a wave. I don't want to start crying in front of anyone.

"You okay, Gabi?"

"I'm fine. Gotta run. Catch you later."

I turn the corner and race to my locker.

Why does Raf Barron make me feel all the things?

I take a long bath after my homework is done and when the doorbell rings, I sit up. *Ashton.* Dammit!

When I open the door, Ashton is holding a huge bouquet of red lilies.

The smile instantly drops off of his face. "What are you doing with those?"

"They were on the front step. Here, see who they're from."

"You didn't bring them?"

"No...they were there." He points at the same spot on the porch where I found them before.

I don't see anything else suspicious. My hands shake when I take the flowers from him and he frowns.

"Hey, what's going on?"

"Why don't you tell me? I don't know what you're up to, but I didn't sign up for all of this between you and Raf. Why are you acting like we're a couple?"

"Would that be so bad?"

"It's not true. It's like an act you put on when you know he's watching. Stirring up trouble. I don't know why we're pretending to be anything different than what we are. We're friends, right?" I shut the door and walk to the kitchen, putting the lilies in the trash.

"Why are you throwing those away?"

"I hate lilies."

His eyebrows lift to the ceiling. "Remind me to never give you lilies."

"Seriously, *I hate them*."

He holds up both hands. "Okay, okay. I was impressed they weren't roses. Who are they from?"

"I don't know."

"You didn't see a card with it?"

"There was no card."

"But you know who they're from...which is why they're in the trash."

I put my hand on my hip and glare at him. "Quit avoiding my questions...what is your deal with Raf?"

"I just think he needs a little push in your direction. His jealousy with you...I've never seen him like this. He's my friend, even though he's being the biggest asshole there ever was right now, but I know him better than anyone and he deserves to let someone in. He never has, you know."

"Seems fine letting Heidi Serrin in."

He makes a face, scoffing exaggeratedly. "She is a piece of meat he did a while ago and never looked back. One and done."

"That's supposed to make me feel better?" I groan.

"Well, yeah. He could have anybody, as many times as he wants, and he is hot after you."

"I still don't know how this little game you're playing is helping anything."

"Maybe it's a distraction for me too," he says, leaning against the counter. "Maybe I need to see how much he wants you."

All of the energy is sucked out of the room and Ashton sags, like the weight of the world sits on his muscular shoulders. I lean over and put my hand on his arm.

"Ashton? What is it?"

"I love him," he says simply.

When I step closer, he avoids looking at me and I shift so he can't avoid me. His eyes fill with tears.

"Oh," I whisper.

"Yeah." He presses his lips together and stares up at the ceiling, blinking fast. "Oh."

"So all those times you were checking me out, you were just playing a part?"

"I can still appreciate an incredible rack." He shrugs, laughing when I flick him. "It's hard *not* to look at your chest, and I have felt more stirring with you than I ever have with any other girl, but yeah...still not like I feel when I see Raf."

I step back and fall into the closest kitchen chair. "I didn't see that coming."

He snorts again and moves to sit next to me. "If I can't have him, I at least want to see him happy. The guy is straighter than a ruler. And he can never know about me. No one can."

"Why not? What would be so bad about everyone knowing?"

"I want to play football professionally. There are a few out men playing, but none of them were out when they were signed. You think anyone would take me if they're afraid I'm gonna bring that press to the field? There's a reason it's kept quiet until a career is established."

"I don't like that at *all*, but I understand why you're protective of your career. You have every right to handle this exactly as you want to. But with Raf...I think you're going about his happiness the wrong way. I don't believe he's interested in me. Fucking me? Maybe. He's a guy. Fucking me *over*? Absolutely, no question. He wants me out of here, Ashton."

He frowns and props his elbows on the table. "But why?"

"That's what I keep asking him. If he ever tells me, you'll be the first to know."

CHAPTER ELEVEN

I get a text from Ashton later that night. We talked for hours and I think I officially have my first friend at Longlake. All reservations I had about not trusting him left the minute he confided in me.

Ashton: You never did tell me who the flowers are from and I'm worried about you. You'll tell me if you're in trouble, won't you?

It takes me a moment to think of what to say and I don't come up with a clever response.

Don't worry. I'm fine.

It feels like a lie and I hate that I'm lying to him so soon after his confession to me, but I'm not ready to face what the flowers could mean just yet.

My phone rings as I'm staring at the phone and I sit up, fumbling to hit answer.

"Laura?"

"I'm so sorry I haven't called you back before now. I've had some family things going on...I should've set up another sponsor for you in the meantime, but I've just been…" She lets out a long exhale. "There's no excuse. Are you okay?"

"I will be. Question is, are you?"

"No." Her voice trembles when she says the word and it reminds me that Laura is not that much older than me. She sounds incredibly fragile right now.

"What's going on, Laura?"

"My brother is in the hospital, but he's turning the corner. It's been scary. I've had to talk with my sponsor more than ever…" She exhales a shaky breath. "This is more personal than I'm supposed to be talking with you, but we're friends, right?"

"Of course. I'm so sorry about your brother. Is there anything I can do to help?"

"Just please talk to me and tell me what's going on with you. You haven't been drinking, have you?"

"No, but it's been more tempting lately. My school…it's a hard place to fit in. They don't want me there. There is this one guy will do anything to get me out and I don't know why."

"Have you ever thought he might have a reason for getting you out of there?"

"Uh…no? What possible reason could he have?"

"I don't know…just, uh…just trying to talk it out with you," she stutters.

I frown into the phone. She's acting strange. "You sound like you need a long break, Laura. I'm worried about you. Don't worry about me, okay? Just take care of you and your brother."

"Thanks, Gabriela. Listen, I'm going to text the number of another sponsor…so there's backup if I can't be reached. You'll like her. A nice lady named Jill and she knows I'm giving you her number."

"I'm not losing you as a sponsor though, right? Just right now, when things are crazy for you."

"Yes," she says emphatically.

But when we hang up, I'm shaken by the conversation. I should've made sure she was okay.

Last night, I told Ashton to back off with the touchy-feely approach at school, so I'm curious to see how he'll be today. I think I convinced him that making Raf jealous wasn't the best thing for either one of us, if we don't want to make Raf even angrier than he's been. Hopefully I got through to him. We'll see.

My mom is extra perky as I'm leaving. She's gone out on another date with the same guy and she's being quiet with the details, but it seems like she's excited. I've tried to ask about him and she just says she doesn't want to jinx it by talking about him too soon. The thought of a man around the house doesn't warm my heart. It was a relief when my dad left. The fighting was out of control, his jealousy was over the top, and the way they dealt with me regarding Luke became a point of contention between the two of them.

I've heard from my dad maybe twice since we moved here. My mom doesn't talk to him at all. It's weird how he's dropped out of our lives. I didn't believe he ever would, but I'm okay with it. He was never around all that much, and when he was, I wished he'd hurry up and leave.

With the red lilies showing up and what I've dealt with at school, I've had enough to think about to give my dad much thought, but all this with Raf has made me wonder if I'm chasing what I know. I grew up with a controlling father. Why wouldn't I *run* from a guy who's trying to pull the same act, instead of obsessing over him?

I'm disappointed in myself for not being stronger. There are times I give the attitude right back to Raf, but when he kisses me or touches me, I lose all reason. I'm ashamed that I'm this weak.

I don't want to think about what my dad will do when he knows my mom is dating again. The fact that they're divorced might make all the difference, but it's giving me one more thing to be anxious about. I haven't told my mom about the flowers and I don't want to.

I drive myself to school and park across from Raf's car. He still hasn't gotten it fixed and it's a constant reminder of my first interaction with him. I should've run then.

I'm weary when I reach my locker and again, stand as far back as I can just in case something is waiting to fly out. Nothing does, but this time, there are pictures posted all over the walls of my locker. All sex scenes. A picture falls out and I gasp. It's a picture of my mom in a horrifying position, every body part on full display. The picture is grabbed before I can reach it and I look up to see it in Heidi's hands as she studies it, the grin stretching across her face.

"Well, well, what do we have here? Looks an awful lot like you, but not quite...the apple doesn't fall far from the tree." She steps closer and waves the picture around, getting in my face. "Didn't take long for your little whore pedigree to come to light."

Raf stands past her, a few feet away, listening to every word. His expression dares me to turn this into a war.

"Did you do this?" My voice catches so I don't say anything else.

Why? Why would he or anyone else do this? Heidi I

can kind of understand, but with Raf's whore comment, it seems more likely that it's him.

I snatch the picture out of her hands and shrug, tossing it back in my locker before slamming the door. "My mom still holds the title for the highest paid porn star. It doesn't take a genius to figure out who she is." I point at Raf and the color drains a bit from his face. "Raf met her when he came over, so looks like the guy you're wanting so badly has a thing for MILF porn."

Heidi glances back at Raf and flushes, not liking the direction this is going. I'm not broken enough for her, not *dismayed* that the truth is out.

"I wouldn't be surprised if there are videos of you too," she says loud enough for me to hear.

That does get to me, but I hold my head high and lean close enough to see her dilated pupils. "Stay out of my business."

Her eyes burn and she doesn't look scared at all. Ashton comes around the corner then and he hustles over when he sees that Heidi is in my face.

"Go away, Heidi," he says. "Quit creating drama where there is none."

She cackles. "There's plenty of drama where this one is concerned."

But she walks off and I sag into Ashton as he hugs me. "You okay?"

"Not really, but I will be."

"Come on, let's get to class. Ignore that bitch."

When I pull away, Raf is still standing there watching. He looks like he wants to hit something and I can't help but grin when I walk by.

"That didn't exactly go as you were hoping, did it?" I

shoot up my middle fingers and turn around, feeling the heat of his anger on me as I walk away.

"Well played. I didn't see the picture, but I heard enough to get the gist. Care to explain any of this to me?" Ashton says.

"I'll tell you. Tonight. I think it's already out anyway."

CHAPTER TWELVE

It's a long day of pointing and laughing and jeers and pranks and just a general hellishness that feels endless. The worst is when I go to my locker after lunch and find a packet of coke, front and center. I glance around to see who is watching and don't see anyone suspicious. I take it to the bathroom and flush it down the toilet. When my locker is searched by the principal fifteen minutes later, I hope to God I got it all out in time. Good thing I cleared the pictures out earlier.

Fuck me.

"I apologize for this search, Ms. Sinclair. It was brought to my attention that you have drugs in your locker and that you've been seen doing drugs on more than one occasion." Mr. Saunders tries to stare the truth out of me.

"That's just not true. I don't do drugs."

His lips are pinched in condescension and I wonder how much he knows about my time in rehab. I'm telling the truth, though. My vice is alcohol. What I wouldn't give for a water bottle filled with vodka right now.

"Well, I hope you don't prove me wrong."

He walks away and I sag against the locker, taking deep breaths until I'm somewhat calm.

If it weren't for Luci and Ashton, I don't know how I'd get through this day. Jen and Melanie tripped me in gym and I have a bloody knee from it. The common thread is everyone knows about my mom and they think I must be just as slutty.

I see Ashton yelling at Jen later and she looks at me guiltily over his shoulder, but she doesn't apologize.

Raf stays one step removed, hovering with his watchful eye but keeping his hands clean. I'm sure it's all his doing. He warned me things would get worse if I stayed. The question is, why does he want me to leave so badly?

When I reach my car, I'm ready to sink into the seats and have a long cry on my drive home. But my back tire is flat, the nail someone used to do it lying on the ground in defiance. I don't waste time trying to fix it. I ask my mom to call AAA and I walk to the field to watch Ashton practicing while I wait for a truck to show up.

I don't know football at all, but Ashton seems to know what he's doing. I decide to make more of an effort to come to his games. He's been a good friend to me, it's time I do the same in return.

The AAA truck arrives and they fix my tire. It would've taken me forever to do it and I didn't feel like being on display any longer. By the time I get home, I see my mom and a man talking out on the sidewalk by the mailboxes. He's tall, so familiar. It hits me as soon as I see his icy blue eyes. Raf's dad. Has to be. I've never seen him before, but I'd know him anywhere. He's the hot older version of Raf.

He laughs at something my mom says and she reaches out and holds onto his arm as she laughs. They're awfully familiar with one another. My eyes narrow on the way he moves in closer to her. They both look at me when I inch the car closer to them, pushing the button to make the passenger side window go down.

"Oh, J-Gabriela," my mom says, jumping when she sees me. "This is Stefen, our neighbor. You haven't met yet." She swallows hard and looks at me with guilty eyes.

I lift a hand and Stefen leans into the window. "Hi Gabriela. It's nice to meet you. Raf says he's in a couple classes with you."

"Did he?" My words come out with more bite than I intended and my mom gives me a sharp look. Maybe she thinks it's because I caught her flirting, and I haven't fully worked through that yet—has she already ditched the guy she's dating?

They have no idea how much I hate Stefen's son right now. Especially if he's pretending like we're buddies to his dad.

"He can be a little asshole," Stefen says, laughing. "Your mom just realized the two of you go to school together." He runs his fingers through his hair and glances back at my mom. They share a look and I groan out loud. This is definitely not their first time to hang out.

"I didn't realize when I met him that he was—" her words trail off. "Raf and Gabi are *friends*, right?" she asks pointedly.

"No," I say between gritted teeth.

I guess I don't have to worry about her trying to set me up with Raf anymore. It's as if the thought makes her sick now.

"Ah, I'm sorry to hear it. We'll have to work on that," Stefen says.

Hell no, we won't be working on that.

"I'll let you get inside. Your mom said you had quite the day with a flat and all."

"Looks like she had quite the day too."

He stiffens, uncomfortable. He knows he's in the middle of something but isn't sure how to get out of it. He lifts a hand and smiles and I slam my car door and go inside.

My mom comes in about fifteen minutes later and finds me in my room. Her hand is on her hip before she ever gets a word out.

"Do you want to explain your attitude, Josephine?"

"Is that the man you're seeing?"

"Why would that matter?"

"Is he or not?" I yell.

"You lower your voice. What is your problem?"

"You couldn't pick anyone other than Raf's *father*?"

"I didn't *know*." She moves her hair off of her shoulder, her face flushing. Guilty. "But would it matter? Are the two of you dating?"

"There are so many reasons it matters. And you were dying for me to date him before you knew, admit it. What if I am?"

"Are you?" she whispers. And for a moment, I wish we were just so I could see what she'd do about it. I sigh.

"No, we're not."

She sags with relief and I roll my eyes.

"Does Dad know?"

Her face changes from relief to terror in seconds. "No. And he can't know."

I take a deep breath, trying to get my panic to subside. No, Dad can't know. Ever. "I'm assuming Stefen knows about Sookie?"

"Well, yes. I didn't want to start a relationship with lies."

I groan and throw my backpack on the floor, glaring at the ceiling as I fall back on my bed.

"You're being overly dramatic, Josephine. If the guy I'm seeing can accept my past, you should be able to too." She gulps hard and her eyes fill with tears. She still feels responsible for what happened with me, and I know I shouldn't let her, but I partially blame her for it too. "You can't hold my career against me forever, sweetheart." A tear falls down her cheek and I sigh, reaching out for her hand when she sits next to me on the bed.

"This morning when I got to school, my locker was full of pictures of you in different...positions."

She gasps and slams her hand against her mouth. "What? Who would do that?"

"You're the only one out of the two of us who has told anyone since we came to town...I'll give you one guess."

My mother fumes and paces across the floor, threatening to go to Stefen's house to confront his son about his abhorrent behavior and then the school when I refuse to let her.

"I don't understand why Raf would do this. I thought you guys were friends."

"I admitted in front of his father that we're not."

"But he seemed so nice when he was over here that day."

"He's had it out for me from day one and I wonder if it got worse when you started dating his dad."

"Well, you stay away from him. I won't be going out with Stefen again."

"I can tell you like him."

"I do, but I won't have you bullied by his son. I need to talk to him about this...just to give him an explanation."

"Not tonight. Okay? Just...let me get through this day. It was awful. My school is the worst."

"What about Ashton? He's such a sweet boy."

"He *is* a sweet boy...who likes mean boys. Particularly Raf Barron."

"*Oh.*"

"Yeah, *oh.*"

We fall asleep talking and I wake up in the middle of the night as she's getting up to walk back to her bedroom.

"I'll make this right, Josephine," she whispers. "Don't worry. I'll fix everything."

The school is abuzz with something besides me the next day, and I couldn't be more grateful for the distraction. And it's good news. Apparently, Toby Matthison has woken from his coma and is expected to recover. News about him has been about how I assumed it would be—everyone cared when the drama was at an all-time high, but since he was never super popular, no one has kept the same level of emotion and the topic has died down. But today, the news is circulating and it's enough to get the focus off of me.

It reminds me that I should check on Laura. She's been quiet again and she'd mentioned her brother being sick. I should see if he's okay. I call her during my break and she picks up, sounding much better than the last time we spoke.

"Are you okay, Gabi?"

"I am. Getting through each day. But I've been worried about you? How are things going?"

"Well, I'm happy to say my brother is out of the woods. The doctors think he'll make a full recovery. He's young...not quite 23, so he stands a chance of being back to himself soon."

"I'm so glad to hear it. That's great news, Laura!"

"Thank you. I know. I'm so relieved. Hey—did you ever give that other sponsor a call?"

"No, I've been dealing with things on my own. But I can if I ever get in bad shape again."

"Just call me. I think my schedule will get back to normal now that I'm not with Toby all the time."

I frown. How many coincidences could that be? Her brother is in a coma and finally recovering...and named Toby? But she said he's older. I remember being at the coffee shop with her that day and she got a call. *That's where I know Toby's face.* His picture came up on her cell phone. What the hell?

"What caused his coma?" I ask, my heart pounding harder. I don't know what's going on, but something is all kinds of wrong about this.

"It has to do with his job. He has a dangerous one," she adds. "Look, I've gotta run. He's waking up and he'd kill me for talking about him. Everything is so hush-hush with him, I shouldn't have even said what I did. I don't know the half of what he does, so I should keep my mouth shut. I'm just so glad to have him back."

"I'm happy for you."

We hang up and I stare at the empty halls, wondering what is going on. Why would a twenty-three-year-old be at Longlake as a student?

CHAPTER THIRTEEN

I go for a run early the next morning. I hate running, but I haven't been dancing or gardening or anything physical since I got here, and my mind and body are sluggish. It's a mistake because as I get too far to turn around, I see Raf running toward me. Instead of moving past me, he turns and joins me.

I stop and face him. "You're not welcome on this run."

"When has being welcome ever stopped me?"

"How long have you known our parents are dating?"

"Long enough."

"You must hate your father...to be exposing his girl-friend like that to Longlake, where reputations go to die."

He doesn't deny it and when I start jogging, he moves alongside me.

"My father doesn't deserve a girlfriend."

"Well, my mom deserves someone kind. She's been dealt with enough bad relationship juju to last a lifetime, so I guess it's a good thing they're going to break up."

"Can't say I'm sad about that," he says.

"You're a cruel person, Raf." I don't know if I'm breathless because I'm running faster or if it's what I'm saying and who I'm saying it to. Tears blur my vision but I keep going. "I *hate* you."

He yanks my arm, pulling me to an abrupt stop before dragging me to a tree with a low covering of branches. He pulls us underneath the covering and leans down, his face in mine.

"I told you it would get worse. I told you to get out of here. You won't listen."

His eyes drop to my lips and in the next second, his hands are in my hair and he's kissing me like I'm his last best chance for living. His tongue clashes with mine and I groan. He tugs my waist toward him and thrusts, his erection hot and long against my stomach. The next thing I know, my legs are around his waist and he's lowering me into the dirt, the shadows from the branches creating a dappled effect with the sun. His mouth travels down my neck and to my breasts and I feel like I'm being consumed by him.

A noise in the distance makes me jump. The sound of a child playing nearby. I push him back, but he keeps traveling down, his fingers getting closer to my weakness. I pull his head up and he comes back to my mouth, kissing me hard and thrusting into me.

I hear the child again and I knee Raf in the nuts. He pulls back, the rage immediate.

"What the fuck?"

I expect him to shove off of me, but it's like an aphrodisiac. He pulls my yoga pants down and thrusts two fingers inside of me. I'm so sensitive, I come immediately and the smug look on his face is my undoing. I hate myself almost as much as I hate him. He pulls his sweats down and I don't look. I know I'll like what I see way too much. He teases me with the tip and I keep my eyes closed, biting my lip hard.

And then everything goes cold. My skin pebbles with goose bumps and I feel the loss of his warmth. I open my eyes and he's gone. I sit up and pull up my pants, my humiliation complete. I stay there for a few moments, blasting myself with all the ways I've screwed up.

I keep letting him break me down. Something has to change. I refuse to keep being his pawn.

The red lilies are on my front step every day for the next week. On day seven, I yell and tear them apart and my mom comes running out the front door with a baseball bat.

"What's going on?" She bends over at the knees when she sees I'm not hurt or being mugged.

I hold up the ripped flowers and her eyes widen when she sees the mess on the ground.

"Did you see who left them?"

"No, but it's happened a lot. Every day this week...other times before that. Is Luke here?"

She gets antsy and I know what she's going to say before she says it. "I don't know. I've heard from my investigator that he was in jail and then got out..."

"So that was about Luke."

"What?"

"I overheard that conversation and was trying not to be nosy, but I should've been...or you should've *let me know*," I yell.

"Keep your voice down. I need to talk to Stefen about this. See if he's seen anything."

"Right, I'm sure that'll help." My mom flinches like I'm smacking her with my sarcasm. "You've been moping around the house for days...I'm sorry you're missing your boyfriend so much. You may as well go back to him. Raf and I aren't speaking anymore. We've avoided each other all week. It's the best week I've had at school...if this with the lilies didn't keep happening. There's no risk of a stepbrother love affair going on at this point. You're safe."

The image of us under the tree has played in vicious loops until I feel like I'm losing my mind. But at least it's not happening again.

Tears stream down Mom's cheeks and she picks the flowers off of the ground and dumps them in the trash, holding the door for me after we've picked it all up.

"I'm sorry. I shouldn't have said all that." My shoulders drop.

"No, you have every right to be upset with me. I should've never had a child while being in the porn business. I should've never introduced you to Luke. Never trusted that his intentions were honorable. Never left you alone with him or alone, period, so much of the time. I shouldn't have stayed with your father as long as I did. All of this is my fault. The least I could do was break up with Stefen." Her voice cracks when she says his name. "He understood. I barely know him anyway." Except now she's sobbing and her shoulders are shaking.

"Mom." I take her in my arms and hug her tight, feeling more like the parent than ever. "If you miss him that much, call him. It's not that big of a deal."

"I can't do anything right," she whimpers.

I roll my eyes and take a few deep breaths before saying anything. "I know it's hard to believe, but not everything is about you."

She stiffens once my words are out and pulls away, her eyes flashing. "I know that."

I press my lips together and my eyes widen, wanting her

to think about it for just one second, the possibility that she manages to turn everything around to herself.

Thursday after school, Luci and I hit the closest coffee shop. We have a science test coming up and it's not my best subject. However, little studying has been done because we've been discussing at length how we feel about K-pop. She's for it, I'm not as much.

"I just don't see what the big deal is." I put my chin in my hands and she stares at me in disbelief.

"I can't believe you don't understand it!"

"I'll keep trying." I shrug but deep down I know I've given it a solid try. I don't want to ruin her fun though. I wouldn't have told her how I felt if she didn't continuously ask how I feel about certain songs and I have to keep admitting I don't know them. And then when I do know the song and it's not my favorite, apparently my expression gives me away.

She goes into this long tirade about it being more than their songs, it's the feeling behind the music, and I lose my ability to concentrate and stare out the window. I jump when I see someone who looks just like Luke staring at me from across the street. I stand up and turn around, quickly stepping away from the window before peeking back out there.

"Uh, what are you doing?"

He's not out there when I look again. I stand fully in the window then, searching both directions.

"I must have imagined it. I thought I saw someone I used to know."

"Someone you like?" She frowns. "Because you look terrified right now."

I run my hand down my neck and take a deep breath. "Someone I hoped I'd never see again."

"Tell me everything." She leans in as I sit back down.

"I...I'm not ready to talk about it yet. It's...he's someone who brought out the worst in me and my family. He's the reason my mom and I moved across the country—well, one of them. He ruined my family." I press my lips together and a shudder crosses my spine.

Luci reaches out and takes my hand. "It's okay. Maybe you imagined it was him. Do you see him now?"

I shake my head. I'm not imagining anything. Luke is here. And it's only a matter of time before he comes to get whatever he's after.

I don't tell my mom about seeing him. I make sure the doors are locked every night and I look obsessively on pound websites for a dog that could protect me.

CHAPTER FOURTEEN

All it took was my permission for my mom to start seeing Stefen again. She's floating around the house again and swears that my trouble with Raf is over. I'm starting to believe her. Since the day on the beach, he won't even look at me.

I miss his eyes on me.

He will never know it.

I thought his hatred was the worst thing, but it turns out that his indifference is far worse.

Heidi walks by while I'm closing my locker and she cocks an eyebrow, far too smug for my liking.

"Looking lonelier every day," she pouts. "Turns out your porn star mother didn't teach you all her tricks on how to satisfy a man." She runs her tongue around her candy red lips and simulates a hand job.

My mind runs away with me at the thought of Raf turning to her since he's leaving me alone. It's what she wants me to think. Every chance she gets, she's saying things like this, trying to poke the bear.

I walk past her like I haven't heard her and it's not

enough of a diss, but I know she hates thinking she's not affecting me.

Luci falls into step next to me. "You going to the game this week?"

"Yes. Wanna go—?"

"Stay away from the game," Raf says as he passes us. "Off-limits. Don't push me on this."

He keeps walking while Luci and I stare after him. I'm shocked he spoke to me.

"What is his problem?"

I shake my head. "So many things, but I'm not letting him keep me from the game. I promised Ashton I'd come... Raf can eat it."

She laughs and I do too, but dread and anticipation wrestle inside at the thought of defying him.

I'll be ready for him this time.

I don't bother with school colors. I have no school spirit for Longlake. But I do paint Ashton's number—56—on my cheek. I have a tight sweater and my favorite jeans on and when Luci shows up, she's decked out in navy and green, school spirit from head to toe. She wrinkles her nose when she sees my outfit, but I turn my cheek to the side and point out the number painted on my face.

"Okay, that's more like it. You could've at least worn *one* of the school colors."

"Longlake doesn't deserve my allegiance."

She shrugs. "Fair enough."

"You ready?"

Mom knocks on my door and when I open it, Luci gasps. I turn toward her, surprised to see the awe on her face when she sees my mom. She flushes and holds out her hand, and my mom shakes it, laughing.

"Well, hello. I'm Sarah, and you must be Luci."

"Such a huge fan," Luci says.

"God, Luci! You never told me that."

She grins and ignores me. "The way you broke society's perception of pornography...made it more of an art form. Huge, *huge* fan," she repeats.

I roll my eyes as my mom titters with the attention.

"I'm not sure how I feel about a high school student being so familiar with my work, but it's nice to hear." Mom's cheeks are pink and she presses her lips together, giving me wide eyes.

"On that note, we're gonna go. This is weird." I grab a jacket and my phone, tucking my license and cash in a wristlet.

We get to the car and I turn to Luci. She holds up her hands. "Sorry. I couldn't help myself."

"How did I not know you were such an avid fan of my mother's?"

She bites her bottom lip and cringes as we get in the car and buckle up. "Did I come on too strong? I guess I thought it was something you might not want to know, but yeah..." She lets out a breathy exhale and I shake my head staring at her and holding up my hand.

"No, do not go all breathy when we're talking about my mother."

"If she wasn't your mother, you'd be in awe. Just sayin'."

"I don't want to know this," I yell.

She starts laughing and eventually I join in. By the time I pull into the school parking lot, we're in hysterics. I wipe my eyes and can't even look at her without laughing. I open the door and the blast of cool air reminds me to grab my jacket. I reach in the backseat to grab it and when I turn back around to step out, Raf is standing there, blocking me.

"Why do you insist on being so difficult?"

"You don't get a say in what I do." As tricky as it is to get out of the car with him so close, I manage. My chest hits his and both of us take a quick intake of breath. It makes me feel a slight bolt of power and I stand taller. "Step away."

He holds his hand out as if leading the way. "Remember I warned you. Go home. Nobody wants you here." He leans down in my face. "I can't make it any clearer than that."

I frown up at him. "I'm so tired of *this* game. You and me. I'm over it."

"This is no game. *You don't belong here.*" His jaw clenches and he steps back.

I hold up my fingers. "Toodles. You don't get to decide where I belong."

Luci and I make eye contact and giggle, the high from our car ride barely diminished. I loop my arm through hers, glad to have a friend by my side.

"Ignore him. We won't let him ruin our fun," she says. "Come on. Let's get something to eat right away and find our seats."

I feel Raf's eyes on me and give my hair an extra toss. "Done. Raf, who?"

We laugh again and I feel a hand on my elbow, turning me around. Whatever was contained in him a minute before is gone.

"Are you *drunk?*" he spits.

My brows join in the center, everything in me scowling at him. "No, I am not drunk. What is your fucking problem? Let me go."

He drops his hand and shoves it through his hair. In the

next second, he leans in and studies my eyes, as if he doesn't believe me. He actually sniffs me and I want to hit him.

"I am *not* drunk," I repeat, my voice quiet this time.

Does he know about my stint in rehab? He's acting like it. What else does he know?

He turns without another glance and stalks away, his shoulders tense.

"He just gets crazier," Luci says. "You're *not* drunk, right? Because I should've driven if you are."

"Don't you start too." I walk away, moving toward the concession stand.

"Hold up, I was teasing. I know you're not. I haven't heard you laugh like that *ever*, but I know you're not drunk." She bumps my elbow and I reluctantly grin back at her.

We get our drinks and sit as close to the field as we can. When the game starts, I do my best to follow, but it's a struggle. Ashton plays well, and he makes it easy to focus on him...until the fourth quarter. A group of girls moves behind Luci and me and it only takes a second to hear those whiny voices to know that it's the lame squad led by none other than Heidi. The smell of weed becomes overpowering and I turn around, frowning when a long stream of smoke is blown my way.

Heidi lifts both shoulders. "You looked like you could loosen up." She leans forward and whisper-shouts, "Found any coke in your locker lately? I heard porn stars are quite the cokeheads. Is that where you adopted the habit? Your mom?"

I stand up and pour my drink in her face. She sputters and I grin.

"That's better. Keep the drugs to yourself. I don't want it." I take off down the bleachers with Luci on my heels.

A deafening cheer sweeps over the field and I see Ashton do yet another amazing play. The time runs out and we've won. The team crowds around him, lifting him up. I hang around a little while, unsure of what to do now. I want Ashton to know we came, but I don't want to bother him. When the team runs off of the field, he sees me standing on the sidelines and jogs over.

"You came!" He picks me up and throws me over his shoulder, jogging around in circles.

I smack his butt and laugh. "Put me down, you stinky boy!"

He laughs and acts like he's going to drop me just to hear me squeal. He sets me down and holds onto me as I try to stand up straight. "Wait for me? I'll shower and then we can go to the party at Henry's house. You in?"

One glance at Luci's hopeful face and I know we're going to the party. At least it's not at Raf's house.

"You think it's a good idea for me to go? I threw my drink in Heidi's face earlier."

"Oh shit." He laughs. "Can't stay out of trouble for even one game, can you?"

"Hey, it's been a decent week. We were due a little scuffle, I guess."

Raf won't be happy if I come to the party, which makes me want to go more than ever. His words echo in my head: *You don't belong here.* But Ashton and Luci are smiling, anxious to hang out and it makes me feel better. I shouldn't need Raf's approval, but it will take effort not to care.

"You need a ride?" I ask.

"Yeah. Give me ten minutes."

I tell him where we're parked and Luci and I walk to the car and wait for him inside. The parking lot slowly clears out and it's fun to people-watch from the safety of the car. I check the time and tap on the steering wheel, antsy. It's been more than ten minutes.

A car pulls in and stops a couple of rows from me. I can tell it's a guy in the driver's seat, but it's too dark to see who it is. I see Jen and Amber walk over there first and then Melanie and Heidi follow. Heidi sticks around longer than Melanie and something is exchanged Heidi and the driver. She glances around to see if anyone is watching. I should duck, but I don't. Hopefully she didn't notice us.

"Do you recognize that guy?" I ask Luci.

"No. I don't remember ever seeing the car either."

The car peels out and Heidi saunters over to Jen's car. She gets inside and they leave. I don't want to be at a party with her, but I don't want to let Ashton down.

He climbs in the backseat and pounds the back of our seats. "Let's go. Henry lives one street over from me."

The music is pounding when we step out of the car. The houses are spread out, so maybe no one will complain about the noise.

"What's the story on Henry's parents?" I ask Ashton on our way inside.

"They're nice. Still married to each other, seem to like each other, so you know, bizarre. But they're nice. You'll meet them. They're always around, but it's strangely not uncomfortable."

Now my curiosity is piqued. We step inside and the music is ten times louder. I feel it in my chest and it's hard not to move with it.

"I'll get you guys a drink," Ashton says. "And then we're dancing." He points at me and I make a face.

"Water for me."

He grins like I'm joking and I shake my head. He pouts and Luci and I stand against the wall awkwardly watching the few who have already started dancing. By the time Ashton gets back with water for me and a pink concoction for Luci, the room has filled even more.

Henry's mom walks by and stops when she sees me. "I've never seen you at these parties. I'm Amina Young, Henry's mom."

"Nice to meet you. I'm Gabriela Sinclair."

I can tell she's heard about me by the way her eyes shift, but to her credit, she doesn't break her smile. "I hope you enjoy the party."

I can almost hear her also saying, *Stay away from my son. I'll be watching you.*

I wouldn't want my son hanging out with a porn star's daughter either, so I can't blame her much. Good thing I'm not friends with Henry.

Ashton goes back to grab a drink for himself and once he's chugged it, he points at me.

"Time to get freaky with it."

"Does anyone say that...ever?" I let him grab my hand and drag me out in the middle of the couples. I stare at Luci longingly, but Charlie, a guy from her English class, is talking to her and she looks ecstatic about it.

"I think it's time to bring it back." Ashton pulls me tight against him and starts grinding against me when the music gets going. My eyes widen when he turns me around with my back against his chest and we move like we've always danced together.

I let the music take over and dance like I haven't danced in so long. My eyes close and I lift my arms to the ceiling and let the rhythm cancel out every inhibition. One second, I feel a cool breeze against my back, and the next, a hot chest is against mine, hands on my waist.

I look back, knowing something changed and Raf glares

down at me. His body says something else as it seductively sways in time with mine. I choose to keep dancing and let the music heal the damage that has been done to me this year. I lose myself in the beat.

His hands begin to wander, sliding up my waist and just below my breasts before dipping down dangerously low. I feel him harden underneath me and bite my lip, my eyes fluttering open as I stare back at him in a haze. His pupils dilate and his eyes are an indistinguishable color now. I see the lust clearer than ever before and I wonder why we can't do this just once without it going haywire?

His lips move to the shell of my ear and his tongue slides along the edge. "Did it feel like this with Ashton?"

I don't say anything. I keep dancing, not wanting him to ruin this with his words.

He pulls my hair back in his fist, forcing my eyes up to his. He turns me around and tightens his grip so there is no space between us. I clench my legs together. He feels so fucking good against me, I'm afraid I'll dissolve in a puddle if I don't get a grip. What happened to all that resolve I was going to have around him? One touch from him and it's gone.

I blink and shake myself, stepping back in a stupor. I push his hands off of me and bump into the couple dancing behind me.

"I need to find Ashton," I tell him and turn to run out of the room.

CHAPTER FIFTEEN

I've never been so happy to see a weekend. Last night with Raf was intense. I need the two days to recoup before seeing him again on Monday. Ashton comes over Sunday afternoon and before we start a movie, he fans himself.

"I thought you and Raf were going to have sex right there in Henry's living room. Mrs. Young kept stopping herself from stepping in." He snorts and I feel my cheeks heat.

"Does it bother you to see me with Raf like that?"

"Honestly? No. I like you more than I like him right now. He's being such a jackass. I told him off last night."

"What did he say?"

"That he'd told me from the beginning that you were his and to leave you alone." He rolls his eyes. "I told him you belong to yourself, but the minute you told me you're his, I'd bow out." He laughs when my eyes widen. "He didn't like that. He can't believe I'm letting a girl come between us—which I'm finding hard to believe too, trust me. But I told him the second he starts treating you decently, maybe we'll get back to normal too." His smile fades and I scoot closer to him. "I can't keep liking someone who is straighter than that windowpane. When I go to college, I'll experiment the shit out of that school life...with someone who knows how hot I am."

I lean my head on his shoulder and hold his hand. "I'm glad you told me. And thank you for defending me with Raf, but you don't have to. I feel bad enough that you aren't as close as you were."

"I think it had to go that direction anyway," he says.

"Maybe, but I don't want to add to it. I'm embarrassed about the way I lose it when he's around. I have to keep my head straight until next fall too. I'll have a few months away from him and Columbia will be a whole new start."

"The not drinking—is that a thing or do you just not want to get in trouble for underage drinking?"

"It's a thing."

"Ahhh. Okay, noted." He gives my hand a squeeze and smiles, his eyes lighting up. "Hey—not the best moment, but I've been dying to tell you something and this will definitely be a solid mood enhancer. You're gonna love me so much more for this."

I turn to face him, laughing at the way he's trying to cheer me up. "I already do love you more."

"You'll *really* love me now. Are you ready?"

I nod.

"I got tickets for us to see *Hamilton*..."

"Nooooooo. How is that possible? They're always sold out!"

"A friend of my mom's isn't able to go and she sold me two tickets."

"Your mom didn't want to go?"

He waves his hand. "No, she's not into that scene and I know how bad you've been wanting to see this."

"Oh my god, I can't wait. When?"

"This Thursday night. I've already okayed it with your mom." He grins, extremely pleased with himself.

I hug him hard, squealing. "Thank you, thank you, thank you! This is so exciting. Best surprise ever."

Ashton, Luci, and I have been sitting at our own table. Ashton and Raf's relationship is obviously strained, especially after arguing about me. The first day Ashton came to sit with Luci and me, I thought Raf's head was going to blow off.

Since the party, he hasn't stopped glowering. He watches Ashton and me like a hawk, his face mutinous. I don't want to cause more trouble for him and Ashton than I already have, but I think part of Ashton is relieved to have the distance. He's been able to take a break from his feelings and work on getting over whatever it is he still feels for Raf. I get it. I've needed the distance myself, except for me, it's still not enough.

At night, my dreams are invaded with Raf's kisses. The feel of him against me, the way he felt between my legs, his lips on mine. I can't escape him there. And during the day, it takes every ounce of strength in me not to obsess over what he's thinking, what he's doing, is he sleeping with Heidi, does he think about our kisses?

When I'm not thinking of Raf, I'm worrying about Luke. They've both taken residence in my brain and aren't giving me much of a break. That's why it's been nice to have a couple of days to think about something else. I've wanted to see *Hamilton* since it first came out. We were supposed to go as a family before my parents' marriage split wide open.

The day of the show, I leave as soon as school is out and hurry home to get ready. I wear a short black dress that makes me feel sexy and older, with my highest heels. My hair is still holding the curl from this morning and my makeup is heavier than what I've worn to school in a while. When I step back, my hazel eyes pop and the color on my lips make them impossible to ignore. I grin, my white teeth bright against the lipstick.

Mom gets home right before Ashton arrives and she takes a picture of us in front of the fireplace. Ashton says he wants pictures of us too and hands her his phone before putting his hand on my back and smiling wide, winning us both over even more.

It's not just any car but a limo waiting for us outside.

"Wow, you went all out."

"You deserve it," he says.

"Are you trying to make me fall in love with you? Because it's working."

He gives me a side hug and we talk nonstop all the way to the city.

When we pull to a stop in front of a candlelit restaurant, I grab Ashton's arm. "What else are you up to?"

"I heard this restaurant is incredible. Let's see for ourselves."

I feel like a grownup with the driver opens the door and I step out, walking into a fancy restaurant where they're expecting us. We're seated right away and when chilled sparkling water is poured in our glasses, I smile at Ashton.

"You're the best date I've ever had," I say, clinking his glass.

He takes a picture of me and I groan.

"Except for that."

———

The show is even more amazing than I imagined it would be. We float out of there, singing the songs to each other as we walk back to the limo, hand in hand. We get another selfie inside the car—we've done that throughout the night. His idea every time, which sort of cracks me up.

"Since when are you a Selfie-ista?"

"When have we ever looked this hot?"

I laugh and reluctantly nod. "True."

I doubt Raf would ever think of taking a selfie. I guess I'm not the typical girl either because I rarely take pictures and don't post on social media, but it's endearing that Ashton wants to document our night.

"Thank you for an amazing night." I turn to Ashton and squeeze his hand. "I can't remember when I've had this much fun."

We sing all the way home and laugh about everything and nothing. I feel like I'm getting my joy back...it's been so long. I lean back against the seat and look at Ashton. We're about to turn down my street and I'm about to thank him for the zillionth time when his face changes.

He turns to me, gripping my hand hard. "Gabi, I don't know what's going on."

I look out the window and my heart drops. There are police cars and an ambulance in front of my house.

Our driver says, "I can't pull in the driveway. Are you okay to get out here?"

"Yes, thank you," Ashton answers.

I'm out of the car before the driver can get out to open

my door. There are police cars both on the street and in the driveway and when I step through the gate, a cop stops me.

"I live here." I frantically try to spot my mother.

"Okay, calm down, miss. What's your name?"

"Gabi Sinclair."

Ashton stands next to me, his arm around me.

"Where is my mom? Is she okay?"

"I'll have someone come talk to you in just a moment."

"Why won't they answer me?" I turn to Ashton in a panic.

His hand clasps my cheek, his eyes worried. "They'll be right back. They'll tell you if something is wrong."

Stefen's talking to the officers closest to the house and I feel Raf before I see him. When I turn, his eyes make the slow perusal down my body, his eyes darkening when he sees Ashton's arm around me.

"Do you know what's going on?"

"There was an intruder, and they won't let us inside."

"Where is my mom?"

He puts his hand on my arm and I go completely still at the contact. I've never felt so much terror in all of my life.

Just then the front door opens and a stretcher is carried out. I run to be by her side and am held back by another cop.

"That's my mother. Let me see her," I yell.

"Sorry, miss. She's being taken to St. Francis. We're going to need the room in the ambulance. Are you able to get a ride?"

I look around wildly and Raf and Ashton are both standing there. Raf steps forward. "We'll drive you."

I nod and step as close as I can get to my mother. Her eyes are closed and there's blood everywhere.

"I love you, Mom. I'll be right there. Hang on." My voice drops to a whisper. "Please. Please hang on."

Raf drives and I sit in the front, Ashton in the back. Raf doesn't say anything, but he watches every move we make. Ashton is sitting in the middle and has his hand on my arm, trying to get me to calm down. I feel the weight of Raf's judgment and turn to him, exhausted before we ever even get to the hospital.

"I need peace tonight. A break in whatever this war is we've got going between all of us. Okay?"

He gives me a brief nod and glances back at Ashton. They convey something unspoken, but some of the tension dissolves.

Stefen is already in the waiting room when we arrive, pacing the floor. He glances at me and stops, moving toward me but not knowing what to do. He holds his arm out and ends up patting me on the shoulder.

"What do you know about what happened?" I ask.

"Very little. We were supposed to see each other tonight and she canceled over text, which wasn't like her. I didn't think too much of it. She said she wasn't feeling great and I offered to bring food over. She didn't want me to, in case she had a bug. But then she called, panicked, hours later and said someone was in the house."

My eyes fill with tears and when I blink they spill over. Ashton's arm tightens around me.

"How badly is she hurt?"

"She was beaten pretty bad, but I don't know how extensive the injuries are. I called the police as soon as she called and I was still too late when I ran over there. I didn't see anyone."

"Did she say who it was?" I whisper.

"She kept saying *Hugh* over and over again."

I bury my head in Ashton's chest and sob.

"Gabriela? Is it possible that your dad did this?" Stefen's voice is a cold, leveled rage.

I start shaking, hard.

"Dad, enough." Raf pulls me out of Ashton's arms and wraps his arms around me, holding me tightly until I settle. "You don't have to talk right now. We'll figure this out," he whispers.

"Do you know if she said anything else?" I whisper. "I need to talk to my mom. She wouldn't want me to—"

His body tenses and he pulls back, brushing my hair away from my face and wiping the tears away. His face is pure agony and I don't stop to question why he suddenly cares. I bury my head in his neck and let his soothing strokes calm me.

———

It feels like forever before we see a doctor and when he comes out, he heads straight for me. We've moved to the chairs and Raf and Ashton are on either side of me. I stand up and they do too.

"You can come see your mom now," he says. "She has a few broken ribs, a broken nose, and some contusions that are being stitched up now, but no concussion, no other serious internal damage. We'll watch her for the evening. The police want to ask you both questions and I've held them off as long as possible. Just wanted to give you a heads up on that."

He motions to the doors behind him and I see two officers standing outside a door.

"Thank you. I'm ready to see her."

I walk back with the doctor and start crying all over again when I see my mom. She's sitting propped up on pillows and looks terrible. But she smiles and holds out her hand for me to take. I lean over and kiss her hand.

"I'm so sorry this happened."

"I'm okay." She grasps my hand harder and dread sinks to my toes when she stares intently at me. "I need you to stay with Stefen tonight. You can't go home, Josephine," she whispers. "Your father...I had to talk to him about all of this with Luke and he's in town. I pushed things with him. I told him I'd moved on and—you know how he gets."

My lips tremble and a tears drips into the crevice of my mouth. I blink when I can't see anymore and nod. "It *was* him then...Mom, Stefen suspects Dad."

Horror fills her face and her hand is shaking as she holds on tighter. "He can't. Why would he?"

"Because you were saying Dad's name over and over again when you were found."

She exhales and winces, touching her ribs. "I can explain that away. Don't say a word."

"Why would he do this, Mom? I thought he'd gotten help and...he promised me." It sounds weak even as I'm saying it, but I believed this time would be different. I thought the trauma we went through with Luke got through to my dad and that he wouldn't go down that path with the abuse again.

"He loves me too much." She closes her eyes.

"No. Don't say that. I used to believe you when you said he loves you too much, and now that turns my stomach. That's not love at all. It's violent and cruel. It's the opposite

of love. With Dad and Luke, what was Dad's excuse—
stress? Vengeance for his daughter? But he finds out you're
seeing someone and it's, what—ownership...rage that he
can't have you? When I was little and he got upset at you
for not working with that one actor, the slimy one...what
was it then—your disobedience?" I choke back a sob. "You
have an excuse for every single time he's gone off on you,
but please, *please* do not ever call it love."

Her shoulders are shaking now with her sobs and she
holds her arms out for me. I shift closer to her and hug her,
careful not to hold her too tight. I feel terrible for saying
these things to her now, but how can she still be making
excuses for him? I thought when she divorced him, she'd at
least partially seen the truth.

"You're right, sweetheart. About all of it. I...I need to
reevaluate things."

I pull away and she shakes her head, tears still flowing. I
grab tissues for her and help dab her face around her
bandages.

"I shouldn't be in any kind of a relationship," she whispers. "But, I do need you to go home with Stefen. Just stay
away from Raf."

There's a knock on the door and the nurse sticks her
head inside. "There's a gentleman out here who'd like to see
you. Stefen? Should I send him back or tell him you're too
tired for visitors?"

"Send him back, please."

She nods and backs out of the door.

"Why not Ashton's house? You're friends with his mom,
right?"

A cloud covers her face. "She hasn't called lately...I
think she knows about Sookie and backed off."

"Maybe other things are going on with her. Either way,

I'm sure she wouldn't mind if I stayed over there. I'd feel more comfortable there than—"

"Please don't say a word about your father, okay?" she interrupts.

"Why, Mom? Why are you still protecting him?"

Two raps on the door pause our conversation and we watch as Stefen steps in with a colorful bouquet. His face is anguished as he looks at my mom.

"It's not as bad as it looks," she says, smiling as she continues to dab her eyes. "I get to go home tomorrow, so it can't be that bad, right?" She smiles at the flowers he sets by the side of her bed. "Thank you. They're beautiful."

Stefen leans over and kisses her forehead and the gesture is so tender, so heartfelt, it takes my breath away. I struggle with the lump in my throat. Seeing him treat my mom as if he cherishes her—it's something I've never seen.

It doesn't mean I want to go home with him and I'm hoping to convince her that Ashton's house is a better idea when he leaves, but she jumps the gun.

"Stefen, I hope you're okay with this. I don't feel comfortable having Gabriela at the house. Would you mind if she stays with you? I don't have many friends here, and I trust you."

I stare at my mother, willing her to look at me. How can she trust someone she hardly knows? And after all I've told her about Raf.

"Stefen is a private detective with his own agency," she says, her eyes full of meaning when she looks at me. "He'll keep you safe."

I sink into the seat by the window and let out a long whoosh of breath. A momentary relief. "I didn't know that."

CHAPTER SIXTEEN

Ashton and Raf both stand up when Stefen and I walk into the waiting room. Ashton's by my side first, putting his arm around me, and I watch Raf cringe and look away. I wish it wasn't so awkward between all of us, that Raf knew everything about Ashton...but it's not my story to tell.

"We're taking Gabriela home with us," Stefen tells Raf. And I don't miss the look that passes between them. The *you better not do a thing to mess this up* look.

Raf's jaw clenches and he gives a subtle nod to both of us.

Ashton shakes his head. "No, she should come home with me. Right, Gabi?" He leans in closer, his fingers gripping me tighter.

"My mom asked Stefen to take me home," I tell him. I pat his arm. "I'll be okay," I say under my breath.

Raf scoffs and when we all turn to him, he holds both hands up. "I'll be on my best behavior, I swear."

Ashton glares at him. "So help me, if I hear otherwise—"

"What? You'll what?"

"Guys, this is not the time or place. And remember, you're best friends. You're seriously gonna let a girl come between you?"

All three of us glare at Stefen with that one. I resent the fact that he acts like I'm trying to come between them when all I've ever wanted is peace. He chuckles and waves his finger at all of us.

"Looks like you can at least agree on one thing. Come on, let's get you home." He pounds Ashton on the back. "We'll take care of your girl, man."

Raf growls and Stefen laughs again.

"Oh, to be this age again. I wouldn't go back for all the money in the world."

Raf rolls his eyes and we walk out of the hospital. I hug Ashton and Raf opens the door of his dad's SUV, waiting for me to get in. He shuts the door behind me, never breaking our gaze. Ashton says something to him and he turns around, his shoulders tensing. When he gets in the car, he's radiating anger.

The ride to the house is quiet, except for when Stefen goes through a drive-thru and asks what we want. Raf seems to have calmed down considerably by the time we get to the house and walk into the kitchen.

Stefen sets the bags of takeout on the table and sits down. I dread having a meal with him. I don't know him well. I expect him to have a lot of questions. I glance at Raf and he reaches out to touch my arm but drops it before it makes contact. I swallow hard and he gives a slight nod that reassures me. I sit down and take out the burger. I'm only able to eat a couple of bites.

"Not hungry?" Stefen asks.

"I'm sorry. I can cut this part off and you can have the rest."

"Don't worry about that. There's plenty here. Raf will take you up on that—he's our resident disposal."

Raf grins around a giant mouthful.

I grin. This isn't so bad.

"Gabriela, I'd like to ask you a few questions about—"

"Dad—" Raf shakes his head. "Come on, give her a break. She's been through a lot tonight."

"It's just...the sooner we know who might've done this, the sooner we can make sure she's safe."

"I know, but look at her...she's exhausted."

The lump in my throat grows and I glance at Raf gratefully before turning to Stefen. "You should ask my mom. She knows who did this."

She'd be upset with me for even saying this much, but I'm tired of covering for my dad and letting my mom take the punches.

Stefen's eyes darken and he reaches out and pats my hand. "Thank you for telling me. I had a feeling."

Raf inhales the rest of his burger and mine and stands. "I can show you the guest bedroom. I'll loan you a shirt or whatever you need."

"Thanks." I stand up and try to smile at Stefen. "Thanks for everything."

"I care about your mother. I hope you and I can be friends too."

I don't know what to say to that so I nod and awkwardly follow Raf out of the kitchen.

"Sorry about that," he says as we walk up the stairs. "Sometimes my dad doesn't know when to leave things alone."

"He's a private detective, huh?"

"Uh, yeah. I'm surprised he's already told your mom that. It's not something he usually starts with—women aren't super comfortable with that career choice and it's also risky for too many people to know." He looks at me over his shoulder. "He must trust her."

"She trusts him. Also surprising."

He opens the door to the guest room and it's beautiful with a large bed covered with pillows, a plush comforter, and a soft blanket draped across the end. It's more decorated than his room and fits with the colors in the rest of the house—greys and blues with touches of yellow. "Wow, this is nice."

"We haven't changed anything since my mom died."

My mouth drops and I turn to look at him. He's staring straight ahead. "I had no idea your mom died. When?"

"Three years ago."

"I'm so sorry. I don't even know what to say."

"It's okay. I don't know what to say about it most of the time. Fucking cancer." He stalks to the bathroom and pulls out a towel and washcloth. "I'll grab one of my T-shirts, if you want to sleep in that. If you think of anything else you need, let me know."

"Thank you, Raf."

"It's not Ashton's house, but—" He shrugs and I roll my eyes as he smirks.

I take a long bath and pull his soft shirt over my head. The tears start back up when I crawl back in bed and I sniffle, trying to get a grip and be quiet.

A box of tissues sits on the nightstand and I blow my nose and lie back again, staring at the ceiling. I don't think I'll be sleeping tonight.

The door cracks open and Raf peeks inside.

"You okay, Gabi?"

I sniffle again and sigh. "Not really."

He walks over and sits on the bed. I pull the covers back and scoot over. He crawls in and lies down, staring at the ceiling with me.

"Do you wanna talk about any of it?"

"Why are you being nice to me?"

"I've decided my house is neutral ground."

"Ugh. Okay." The sarcasm in my voice is thick and he laughs, turning on his side to face me.

"Would you rather I pretend we're at Longlake?" His voice is low and raspy and I feel it to my core.

I turn to my side and enjoy the way the light from the window casts just enough on his face that I can see his features.

"I'd never go back to Longlake if I had the option."

"Then quit."

"Why do you want me to so bad?"

"Has it been a happy experience for you?"

"No, but it'll look good for Columbia."

"Columbia, huh? You don't want to go somewhere with more sunshine and heat?"

"Nope."

"Hmm." He reaches out and runs his fingers lightly over my forehead and cheek.

"You're so confusing."

"I think I've been pretty clear. I want you out of Longlake and in my bed."

"Because you hate me..."

"Yes. You're hot. And trouble."

"You hate me because I'm hot?" I gasp when his fingers brush across my lips. When he drags them across again, my tongue sweeps out and licks him.

He groans and does it again and I circle my tongue over his finger, pulling it into my mouth and giving it a long suck.

"Gabi."

"Is this hate?" I whisper.

"Yes," he whispers. "Do you hate me back?"

"Yes," I admit honestly.

"Because I'm hot?"

"Because you hated me first."

He closes the distance between us and when his lips touch mine, I feel the current run through my body, head to toe. His hands drag through my hair and tug, his lips trailing a path from my ear, down my neck, and when he reaches my breasts and latches onto my nipple over the material of the shirt, I arch into his mouth.

"This is a bad idea," I moan.

"We will go back to hating one another more thoroughly tomorrow. My house is neutral," he reminds me, looking up and smiling.

"You're crazy." I watch as he pulls down the neck of the shirt and wraps his tongue around my tip.

"You're beautiful. I've dreamed of this since I first saw you."

"Why didn't you start with that instead of the asshole?"

He sits back and pulls off his shirt before reaching down and pulling mine over my head. I didn't have clean panties so I'm completely bare and I feel my body heat as he stares at me, his mouth dropping open.

"Fuck me. You are so fucking beautiful, it makes me drunk when I let myself fully take you in." He teases my stomach with the tips of his fingers and I shiver. "I'm still the asshole."

"What are we doing?" I put my hands over my breasts and he slides them away.

"Please, let me look. Why would you ever cover yourself up?"

"This changes nothing, does it?" I say it mostly to remind myself, but also because he's acting like he needs reminding. The sweet things he's saying. He doesn't normally go this long without bringing a harsh reality back into our conversations. It will hurt worse if we don't talk it through. I don't want to pretend like we will come out of this any different than what we are: enemies.

"Nothing," he says, licking his lips.

"Take off your pants."

His eyes gleam as he stands up and pulls his sweats down. His cock bobs out, so long and thick that it's too heavy to stand all the way up. My mouth goes dry as all the heat inside of me goes straight between my legs. I lean up, staring at him, his abs, his chest, and back to that weapon between his legs that could do the best kind of destruction to me. He has nothing on any porn star I've ever seen.

"How have you been hiding that all this time?"

He chuckles under his breath and I shudder at the promise in his look. He leans over me and drags me down the bed so I'm lying flat before he lies on top of me. Both of us take a deep breath as we study one another.

"I wasn't done looking at you," I whisper. His erection jerks at my words and I close my eyes, loving the way every part of him feels against me.

"I'll be here all night. You can have your fill tonight only."

"It must feel nice to be the one making all the rules. If I didn't want this right now, I'd shove you off of me so fast, you couldn't see straight. But I'm sad and lonely and you're a body."

Anger flashes across his face and he thrusts against me. "Just a body, huh?"

"Yep. I can be like a guy and not feel a thing for the person I fuck."

He leans away and I pull him back down on me. He stares down at me like he doesn't know what to do now and I arch against him.

"Let's get this over with. You know we just need to get it out of our system."

"Who are you right now?"

"I am your dismantling," I whisper.

His mouth crashes into mine and it feels like an endless struggle of wills. When my mouth feels raw from his kisses, he shifts to assaulting my breasts, sucking, licking, biting them like he can't get enough. His fingers move between my legs, he drags my wetness across my slit and then plunges inside. I can't be still and when he shifts so his mouth is plunging inside of me, I fuck his tongue, my hands in his hair, pulling him as far inside of me as he can go, until I don't know where he begins and I end.

I cry out as the pressure builds and he puts his hand over my mouth, covering my cries as I fall apart. He never stops pulsing his tongue inside and out, covering every inch of my sex until I see stars.

I shudder against him one more time and he leans up, grabbing a condom from the side of the bed.

I'm too dazed to ask if he planned this or just leaves condoms around the house for any opportunity.

I watch as he sheathes himself, admiring the way his hand moves with one long stroke, two strokes...my mouth waters on the third.

Neither of us say a word, but when he slides the tip in, we both gasp and I feel my heart thudding even faster. He watches me, and I can't look away, the intimacy between us suddenly impossible to ignore. I take a deep breath and he pushes another inch in. He pulls back and then slides in further, and one more time before going balls deep. The feeling is out of this world. I close my eyes and arch into him, the hard peaks of my nipples feeling divine against his chest.

"Look at me," he rasps. "I want you to know who's making you feel this way."

Like I could ever forget.

I open my eyes and he pulls out and slams into me again, slowly circling in and out, deliciously taking his time until I'm pulling him into me begging him to move faster.

"Harder," I whimper.

He continues to tease me, dragging across my clit before sinking into me again and again and again until my head is falling back. Eyes rolling back.

"Look at me," he says again.

I force my eyes open and he curses.

"You feel like heaven and hell all at once. Something this beautiful could only be sin." His voice is like a caress and I nearly come again with his words.

He groans and pulls out one more time before slamming back into me. From then on, every plunge into me is hard and fast, deeper, until he reaches the deepest part of me. Our breaths are labored and I scratch my nails down his back, unable to take it for much longer.

It's too raw.

Too real.

Too perfect.

"Come with me," he chokes out. "Come with me so I can get back inside of you and do this all over again."

My insides clench around him tightly and he groans

into my mouth. When I feel him harden right before he comes, I fall over the edge again, and it's the most spectacular feeling I've ever experienced. It lasts forever and we both ride the wave for as long as we can.

His face ends up in my neck and there's a brief awkward moment when he leans back and stares at me again before pulling out. He climbs off of me and walks to the bathroom, coming back a few minutes later and crawling into bed.

We don't look at one another as we catch our breath. But he reaches out and takes my hand and loops his fingers through mine. Just that little bit of contact makes me feel better.

It's not even five minutes later when he puts my hand on his already hard cock and says, "Come over here."

I don't argue. There are some battles I'm willing to fight, and tonight, this is not one of them. I'll deal with the aftermath in the morning.

CHAPTER SEVENTEEN

I wake up to the sun shining right in my eyes. There's a tiny opening through the curtains. The other side of the bed is empty. I ignore the twinge in my chest that feels similar to disappointment.

No, I won't allow it.

I glance at my phone and see that I've missed several texts from Ashton and one from Luci. I slept later than I expected to—it's almost nine. I text them both, letting them know I'm okay and I call the hospital and they put me through to my mom's room.

When my mom answers, she sounds groggy.

"I hope I didn't wake you up. I wanted to talk to the nurse, but they just put me through to you."

"It was a long night. Hard to get any sleep in a hospital."

"Do you think you'll get to come home today still?"

"As far as I know. How are things going over there?"

I picture Raf leaning over me, his eyes memorizing my body as he fucked me from kingdom come and I flush. "It's going well. I haven't gotten up yet, still being lazy, but I wanted to see when I should pick you up."

"Listen, Stefen just walked in. I better go. I'll talk to you soon."

"Oh. What—"

But she's already hung up.

I get up and take a shower and when I step out, Raf is leaning against the bathroom door.

"Who is Luke?"

I frown.

"Who is he?" His face is harsh lines and his eyes slash through me, the memory of last night already distant.

"Good morning to you too. I guess we weren't lying when we said things would go back to normal today."

"Goddamn right. You fuck me one minute and then cry out Luke's name not even half an hour later? You can fucking tell me who he is."

"I would've thought you'd know by now. Seems like you've made it a point to know everything else about me. Or did your investigator father not fill you in on that too?"

He stalks toward me and when I try to tuck the top of the towel so it'll stay together, he yanks it away and it falls to the floor.

"I want one more time with you."

"No." I shake my head, turning from him and facing the mirror. I rinse my face with cold water and dry it off and when I set the towel down, his chest is against my back. His fingers trail down my back and when he reaches my backside, he squeezes before giving it a sound slap. I jolt and glare at him in the mirror.

"Tell me who he is."

"He's no one."

He gives my ass another slap. "Not the correct answer."

"He's from my past."

"Do you love him?"

I scoff, the resentment too deep to even acknowledge his stupidity and he tugs my hair back, forcing me to look in the mirror.

"Did you really think you could give me your body and things could return to normal?"

"Yes. And it seems they have. You're being the same idiot you always are."

"Answer my question."

"No, I do not love him."

His hand loosens in my hair and he runs his fingers down my breast, tugging my nipple. "Do you love Ashton?"

"Ashton is my friend. I love him very much."

His eyes darken but he doesn't stop his movements across my chest. "Have you had sex with Ashton?"

"None of your business."

He pulls my hair back again and nips my neck with his teeth. "Not an answer."

"You don't call all the shots, Raf."

"I do where you're concerned." He buries his nose into my neck but not before I see the smirk he tries to hide. "Bend over."

"No."

"If I put my fingers in your pussy and you're not wet, I will let you go, no more questions. If you're dripping, I will sink into you so deep, you'll forget your name."

My mouth falls open and when he drags his fingers down to my drenched center, I groan loud, my eyes fluttering back. He bends me over the counter and slides a condom on, plunging into me the next second.

We both moan when he's inside all the way.

"Why do you have to fit me so perfectly?" He wraps my

hair around his fist and tugs up, so I will look in the mirror. He pulls out and brings his cock up, tapping it over my clit. It's the hottest thing I've ever seen and I can't look away.

When he thrusts into me again, my boobs bounce with each movement and he looks like a god behind me, fiery and capable of inflicting eternal damnation. I fall apart when his fingers circle my clit and go weak against him.

"Let it out, baby," he whispers. "Let me hear you sing."

I squeeze him so tight, coming so hard, he groans and collapses against my back, convulsing inside me.

When we slow down and I think he's about to pull out, he wraps his arms around me and holds me tight. I look up at him in the mirror and am stunned by the vulnerability in his face. He leans down and kisses my shoulder and I shiver, turning my head toward him. I meet his eyes then and he leans his forehead against mine. It's a brief moment, but it feels like something shifted in that tiny span of time.

He pulls out and throws the condom in the trash, washing his hands afterward. He turns on the shower and holds out his hand.

"Want another since I dirtied you up so thoroughly?"

I step in the shower behind him and watch as he runs his hands through my hair, getting it wet again.

"I love your hair," he whispers.

I swallow hard and put my fingers on his lips and down his neck, his Adam's apple bobbing underneath me.

"What if we didn't hate everything about each other? Would that be so bad?"

"It's impossible to hate your tits," he whispers. "And your ass is the thing dreams are made of."

I laugh, my face flushing with embarrassment. But his words are life. "So basically my looks do it for you but nothing else."

He smirks and I feel his cock bounce up between us. I take the soap and slide the suds over his chest and back, his legs. And when I get on my knees and soap up his cock, I make sure to get it fully clean before I dirty him up myself.

I swallow every drop and know that I have a big problem.

I won't be able to give him up. Ever. Not willingly.

"Your mouth is also excellent...when you're not speaking," he whispers in my ear before we get out of the shower.

"Good thing I can't keep my mouth shut."

I walk out to the bedroom with the towel wrapped around me and my clothes are lying on the bed, clean and folded.

"Thank you," I say when he comes out of the bathroom still naked. I admire his body in the light of day.

God, he's gorgeous. I turn away, already feeling the heaviness of this coming to an end. Whatever this has been.

"I was lying. I know who Luke is. And I know where he is...all the more reason for you to get out of here and leave Longlake."

I tilt my head, speechless. "What do you mean? Where is he?"

He shakes his head. "I can't tell you that."

"Why not?" I snap, stepping chest to chest with him.

"He's working with my father."

I fall back, my legs hitting the bed, as the wind is knocked out of me.

"And if you even *breathe* a word of this to anyone, specifically your mother, it will all be over for both of you. Do I make myself clear?"

I stare up at him and gulp, the tears threatening to surface again unless I can get a grip fast. I stand up, turning my back to him while I put on my clothes.

"I hate you, Raf Barron."

"Good. I hate you too, Gabriela Sinclair."

CHAPTER EIGHTEEN

When Raf goes to his room to get dressed, I go out the back door and am almost to my car when I feel a sharp chill go down my spine. I turn to look over my shoulder and am hit in the back of the head, my vision going black.

When I wake up, I'm in the car and we're speeding through the roads near my house. I turn to see who's driving and groan at the movement but am glad to see that it's Raf.

"You're awake. Stay still. I'm taking you to the hospital."

I hold my head. "My head hurts, but I'm fine. I don't need to go to the hospital."

"We need to get you checked out. Did you see who did this?"

"No. You didn't?"

"He ran when he heard me coming. I saw the back of a guy with a ski mask on. Did he say anything?"

"No," I whisper.

He turns to glare at me and I lean my head against the back of the seat.

"Stop looking at me that way."

"Why were you trying to leave?"

"I wanted to see my mom...and I needed space."

"God, Gabi. You could've been killed. What were you thinking?"

I watch the houses flash by as we drive past. A few more turns and we're pulling into the hospital parking lot.

"Why would your dad be working for Luke?"

"He's *not* working for him," he snaps. "You've got it backwards. Forget I said anything. It's best you stay out of it. I shouldn't have said anything. I hoped it'd be—just forget it."

"How can I forget something like that?"

"My dad said your mom will be discharged soon." His voice is gruff, but it sounds almost like a peace offering.

I'm having trouble getting past the images of the way he looked at me last night versus the coldness he's putting out today.

It's the loneliest feeling in the world.

When he parks, he doesn't move right away. He turns off the ignition and turns to face me. "About last night..."

I hold up my hand and he pauses. "You don't need to say anything about it. We can just pretend it never happened."

His face flushes and his jaw ticks a few beats. "Right. Okay. I'm glad we're...clear on that." He leans down when he sees the sign near where we're parked. "I think we'll be okay here until we can get you checked. Come on, I told my dad we'll be here and can bring your mom home while he goes and checks out your place...if everything is okay with your head."

"It's a waste of time for me to be seen. I've got a lump on my head. No big deal."

He ignores me and steps out of the car, coming around to open my door. I huff inside, knowing I'm not getting out of this and annoyed by everything Raf-related right now. I can't even have the morning walk of shame in peace.

I'm checked in and an hour later, a nurse calls my name.

"Can you go check on my mom while I'm in here?" I ask Raf.

"I'm coming with you," he says, smiling at the nurse.

"No, you're not."

He slides his arms around my waist and nuzzles my neck. I'm stunned into silence. "I have to make sure you're okay, baby. You would do the same for me."

I stare up at him and when he kisses the tip of my nose, it takes everything in me not to kick him in the balls. It would give me warm fuzzies if I thought he meant any of it, but it's all about him having control and I'm sick of it. I don't want to cause a scene with the nurse, so I exhale and follow her. She's swooning over Raf's sweetness and wouldn't notice if I keeled over dead.

A few minutes later, a doctor comes in the tiny room. He tests my eyes and feels around for any weird bumps. He wants to do a CT-scan, but I tell him it's not necessary.

"I didn't want to come. I feel okay. My head is already getting better."

"I'd feel better if we do a scan."

"She definitely needs the scan," Raf speaks up. I roll my eyes and he acts like he doesn't notice.

"It won't take long. Have you had any strange symptoms? Blurred vision, nausea, confusion, dizziness...excessive fatigue?"

"No, but everything went black when I was first hit. I don't know how long."

"Not good," the doctor says.

"It couldn't have been more than a minute or two, but I'm still worried about her," Raf says.

The doctor nods and writes a few things on his chart. "I'll see how soon we can get you back. Jessica will be back to take you," he says and then leaves the room.

Jessica comes in and says the technician is backed up and offers me a drink. I shake my head and she turns to Raf, offering him a drink. Her eyes say that if she could, she would strip him down and swallow him whole. I groan and turn to my side so I don't have to watch her eye-fucking him any longer. I don't blame her. He is so beautiful and now that I know what he feels like...my face flames and I feel my eyes welling with tears. I'm suddenly exhausted. How am I going to survive living next door to Raf now that I've slept with him? It was the best night of my life. I've fallen for the unattainable once again, the worst possible option for me.

Except he makes my feelings for Luke look child's play.

I wipe my tears away quickly, silently cursing myself for getting emotional. It's just too much. I don't know what's going to happen next, but everything is falling apart.

Jessica leaves the room and Raf is quiet for a moment. He puts his hand on my shoulder and I keep facing the wall. I can't look at him.

"Gabi? Are you okay?"

I know if I answer, I'll give away that I've been crying, so I lie still and pretend that I'm falling asleep. He jostles my shoulder.

"Hey, I don't think you're supposed to fall asleep."

When I still don't respond, he crawls into bed behind me, spooning me, and there's no way I could sleep with how awake his body makes me.

He puts his lips to the shell of my ear and when he speaks, liquid rushes between my legs.

"It's going to be okay. We'll find whoever did this." His

lips brush across my skin and hair and he holds me tight, making me feel safer than I should.

My breathing levels out and when they come to take me for the scan later, I'm calm and ready for whatever is next. I don't know how I became dependent on my enemy, but it seems I have. In more ways than one.

———

The results of the scan show no visible signs of a concussion, but to be on the safe side, I'm given pain medication and told to come back if I show any signs of the long list of symptoms Jessica reads off. Nearly three hours after we arrived, I'm released.

We walk upstairs to my mom's room and she's waiting for us, discharge papers in her hand. When the nurse comes back around, she wheels Mom out and Raf runs to pull the car around so she won't have to walk far.

When he pulls up, he rushes around to help her into the car even though I'm there to help her.

"Thank you, Raf," she says.

I turn so she can't see me flush and I get in the backseat. He's right there, helping me like I'm an invalid too. I try to convey with my glare that I don't want my mom knowing I've been in the hospital too, but either he doesn't get the message or he chooses to ignore me.

The first thing he says when he gets in the car is, "Gabriela was assaulted in your driveway."

"What? Gabi? Why didn't you tell me? Are you okay?"

"I didn't tell you because I'm fine. If Raf would've waited two seconds, I could've gotten around to it." I glare at him in the rearview mirror.

His eyes narrow and I shake my head at him, angry that he's butting in.

"Did you see who it was?" she whispers, turning all the way around to try to read me.

My skin is hot and my head is still hurting. I lean my head against the window. "No, I didn't. And I'm fine. No cuts or breaks or concussions..."

"We have to watch her to be sure about the concussion," Raf says.

"Where were you hurt?"

I point to the back of my head and her cheek sucks in on one side, eyes flashing.

"Is that why your dad left in such a hurry and you're the one taking us home?"

"Yes." Raf doesn't elaborate the point and we're quiet the rest of the way. When he pulls up to our houses, he pulls into his driveway instead of ours and I lean up against the backseat to protest.

"Gabi, I've already talked to Stefen about this. We'll stay with them for a few days, at least until it feels safe to go back to our house."

I fall back, too exhausted to fight it. I don't know how to deal with Raf after our night together if I'm in his space non-stop. This is a disaster waiting to happen. And what about our parents? They're going to take one look at my face and know what we did. I just know it.

Raf helps my mom out of the car and leads her to the door. I shuffle out after them and he doesn't give me a backwards glance. It stings a little, the way he can go so hot and cold.

Maybe this won't be an issue at all...if he's a jerk, it should be *no* problem.

CHAPTER NINETEEN

Raf disappears once my mom is settled in the living room. He was completely attentive, getting her a drink, asking her if she needed anything, and making sure she was comfortable...barely glancing at me to see if I'm okay. Which is fine. I need him to treat me the shitty way he's capable of—anything to help me forget the way he worshipped me last night.

My skin flushes again and my mom frowns. "Gabi, I'm worried about you. You don't look so good. Why don't you lie down, sweetheart? Stefen will be back and I need to talk to him about all of this."

"What are you going to tell him?"

"I'm not sure yet."

"Well, let me know when you decide because I don't know which lies I'm supposed to hold onto and which secrets I'm supposed to reveal." My words come out much angrier than I intended and her eyes widen before getting watery. "Mom, don't cry. Okay?" I groan. "I want to go home."

"You can't. We can't. Not yet. Not until it's safe."

"But this is so uncomfortable," I whisper. "I don't even know where to be right now. I'm supposed to be out of the way when you talk to Stefen. You've put me in a house with my bully and expect me to make myself at home."

"Raf was being so sweet earlier," she says under her breath, not quite speaking as low as I think she should. "I think he's sorry for how he's treated you." She smiles hopefully. "Aren't you getting along better now?"

"You know nothing about Raf," I mutter, my eyes getting watery too with the anger I feel. "You know what? I didn't get any sleep last night, so I'm going to find a place to hide and take a nap."

She starts to say something and I hold up my hand, cutting her off.

I go into the kitchen and past that is a sunroom with a cozy chair and a wicker loveseat. It doesn't scream nap to me, more of a place to catch up on a book, but I curl up in the chair, and the next thing I know, I feel something in my hair. I jump and Raf leaps back.

"I didn't mean to scare you. Your mom wants to talk to you and I told her I'd find you. Sorry to wake you." He stares at my mouth while he's talking and the things he did to this mouth play in slow motion in my brain. I shake my head, trying to rattle myself awake.

"Ow." I hold my head. "Okay." I sound groggy and wonder how long I've been asleep.

"You need to take something for your head."

I ignore him. When we walk through the kitchen, Stefen and my mom are sitting at the table with pizzas, clinking their glasses of wine.

"Isn't this cozy," I say under my breath.

"Tell me about it," Raf mutters.

He drags a chair out across the hardwood, letting it

scrape longer than necessary. His dad narrows his eyes at him and Raf sends daggers back, as if daring him to say anything about it. So Raf isn't happy about our parents any more than I am. That's reassuring.

"We would like to talk to you both," Stefen says. "Have some pizza, Gabriela. I hope you're feeling better after your incident this morning."

Raf slides over a bottle of the prescription I was supposed to fill but didn't because we rushed home with my mother. "I filled this for you while you were asleep. Your mom said it was okay."

"Thanks. I'm feeling fine," I tell Stefen.

"Your mom and I have been talking, and I've extended an invitation for you both to stay here with us as long as necessary. She's filled me in on...some of the things I was missing...but we're looking into all the possibilities for your mom's accident, as well as yours."

"I haven't talked to the police—have you, Mom?"

She shakes her head.

"Well, that's weird. Why are we supposed to just trust Stefen to take care of us?" I stare at my mother, but she won't look at me. She's looking at Stefen like he holds her entire world in his hands. I turn to him. "Is it true you're working with Luke?"

My mom turns to me so fast, I think it makes her dizzy. She holds her temples. "It's not what you think, sweetheart."

"It seems someone has been speaking out of turn." Stefen directs that to Raf and the tension is so thick I'm afraid one of them is about to turn the table or something else equally as destructive. "Let me worry about the details, okay, Gabi?"

"It's Gabriela to you," I snap. I stand up from the table

and put a piece of pizza on a plate. "Where can I go so I don't have to have this conversation right now?" I take a bite and I'm not hungry so I regret even eating that much. I force myself to take three more bites so it's not wasted and set the plate down.

"Sit down, Gabi," my mom says.

I ignore her. She exchanges a look with Stefen and shakes her head slightly. I can't believe my mom is trusting this guy when we hardly know him. I'd go to Ashton's just to get out of the same house as Raf, but I can't leave my mom here alone with them.

"We're going to keep you safe," Stefen says. "Both of you have nothing to worry about. My best guards are watching the place, as well as yours, and I can walk through the security system with you after dinner, if you'd like."

"I don't understand why you're keeping this from the police." I lean against the table, still not willing to sit down and pretend like this is normal.

"It's best if you don't know all the details of what I do." Stefen steeples his hands together and looks so much like Raf in this moment, it's hard to think straight.

"Well, this has been enlightening." I roll my eyes. "I'll just go wherever I'm supposed to be sleeping since I'm not getting any answers here. At some point, I'll need to pick up a few things from home."

"If you tell me what you need, I can go get it, or Raf can take you to the store."

Raf puts a couple of slices on his plate and stands up. "Same room as last night. I'll come up with you." Neither of us act like Stefen has spoken.

When we get upstairs, I go to the bedroom and sit on the bed. It's hard to even look at Raf when we're in this room. It's all so fresh and yet in some ways that feels like another lifetime ago.

"I don't want your dad picking out my underwear and clothes."

"I can go get your things."

"Not much better." I shrug.

He sits next to me on the bed. "You'd prefer my dad over me?"

I roll my eyes. "Don't make it weirder than it already is. I...how are we going to do this?" Every part of me feels how close he is right now. I could lean over an inch to the left and my shoulder and thigh would touch his.

"Last night shouldn't have happened," he says.

I know he's right and I even knew he felt that way about it, but it still hurts like hell to hear him say it out loud.

"Obviously."

He takes a sharp intake of breath and I sneak a look at him. His face is unreadable and I wish he'd give me a hint of how he's feeling.

"Why did that happen last night? *All night long*," I whisper the last words.

"We gave ourselves permission to feel the attraction, but that's all this is, and it was just one night." He snaps once. "Done in the morning."

I nod, pressing my lips together. "Right. One and done... or in this case, three and done."

He looks at me then and his eyes are as emotionless as a snake. "It would've been nice to get one more time in before we returned to reality, but..." He shrugs. "That would've been greedy."

"And three times wasn't?"

"Three times is nothing for me in a night. Not for you

either, I'd expect. If anything Luke has told my father about you is true."

I feel a lump forming in my throat. I stand up and stare down at him, slapping him across the face. He holds onto my wrist and stands up, leering over me.

"My past is none of your business. And if you and your father expect us to stay here and figure out whatever this is that's going on, which is craziness, then you'll stay out of my way and stay out of my life. You know *nothing* about me."

"I know plenty. I know how you like it when I fuck you hard and fast and the way you love what this tongue can do. I know that you like sex and I'm not the only one you've liked it with." He shrugs again and I hate him more than ever before. "I know you say Luke's name in your sleep after you've fucked me all night." His eyes are bitter when he says that, and I think perhaps he's not as unaffected as he's appearing to be. "Let my dad do his job and we'll stay out of each other's way. Deal?"

"Get out of this room and don't come back."

"Gladly." He stalks to the door and turns around, smirking. "I have a date with Heidi tonight. I don't think I'll bring her back here. That'd be too insensitive of me, wouldn't it?" His eyes are pure evil as he laughs and opens the door and doesn't bother shutting it as he walks out.

I slam the door and hear his laugh all the way down the hall.

I won't last a week in this house if it's going to be this kind of hell.

CHAPTER TWENTY

My mom comes in later, after I've showered and cried and raged. I don't feel much better, and when she comes to sit next to me on the bed, she doesn't look all that great either.

"What's going on, Mom? Why are we here?"

I thought my tears were gone, but I feel the lump rising in my throat and I try to shut down the emotion.

"It won't be long, honey. It's not safe at our house right now."

"But that's right next door. How can we be any safer here?"

"Stefen is watching out for us and he's going to help us. As soon as things have settled, we'll go home."

"I don't understand what's happening. Is this Dad? Why is Luke working with Stefen? That's a red flag if ever I saw one. Tell me you're not getting involved with another man who's as awful as Dad is."

Her eyes snap and I regret the words coming out of my mouth because I don't want to deal with her waterworks for another second, but...yep, here they come.

"How can you say that when I was the one who got us out of there?"

"After how long? You were married, what, eighteen years?"

She stands up and her shoulders are drooping as she walks to the door. "I know it's too much to ask that you show a little respect for me, Josephine, but I'm trying here. I know I've made the worst decisions, but I'm trying to make the right ones now."

"I wish they didn't involve another man...one that we barely know." My words hit their mark and she straightens, turning around to me with resolve.

"I knew Stefen before we moved here." She focuses on the comforter instead of my face and speaks as if it's torture for her to tell me the truth. "He's the one who actually got us out of Vegas."

She steps out of the room before I can process that bombshell. I should run after her and demand that she answer all my questions, *now,* but I'm too upset and exhausted to move.

I did respect my mom's ability to get us away from Dad and into the beautiful house across the country. Maybe for the first time since I was a little girl, I'd respected her for this. Turns out it wasn't her at all.

And I'm no better than her.

I fell for Raf the instant he seduced me, barely making him work for it at all. *Be cruel to me and I'll still have sex with you if you touch me just right.* Now he has more to hold over my head and I'm just another notch in his belt.

I don't go to school the next day and I don't leave my room. My mom brings me a sandwich and a drink in the afternoon. She eyes me warily as she sets the plate by the bed.

"You feeling okay today?" she asks.

"I'm fine." My head hurts and I didn't sleep, but she's the last person I want to talk to right now. "You?

"Doing okay." She nods. She winces when she reaches out to open the drapes. She must be lying too. "If you're fine, you'll need to go to school tomorrow."

"I'll need my uniform, more clothes for around here, and underwear. And my makeup..." I clench my teeth together and take a drink.

"I'll go to the house with Stefen in a little while. Anything else you want me to grab?"

"I need my laptop and my backpack. You're obviously running this show, so I guess whatever you want me to have." I shrug and take a bite of the sandwich.

She sighs. "It doesn't have to be this way."

"No reason to be upfront and open now, Mom." I chew the sandwich and set it down, my appetite nonexistent. "Just leave me alone. I'm tired. I'll go to school tomorrow, just leave me alone."

I stayed up most of the night listening for Raf and never heard him come back. Earlier, I checked to see if his car was out in the driveway, but I didn't see it. Maybe he spent the night with Heidi and they're all laughing about me at school today.

Ashton and Luci have texted throughout the day to see how I'm doing and to ask if I need anything. Ashton texts again at the end of school.

Ashton: I'm heading out. Can I bring a milkshake over for you?

I'd love that, but I'm just resting another day. I'll be back tomorrow, promise.

I never told him about my run-in with the guy outside my house, so he is still going on the assumption that I'm worried about my mom and struggling to deal with Raf in this house. I don't want to add to his concern.

I get another text a few minutes later from Laura.

Laura: You okay? I haven't heard from you in so long.

I don't say anything for a while. She's usually had a sixth sense for when I'm not doing great but has been out of the loop since everything happened with Toby...which is still bothering me.

For the first time since moving here, I long for the familiarity of Vegas. I might not have had a normal life there either, but I had favorite bookstores and coffee shops that I loved. Things weren't good at home, and when it got nuts with Luke, I at least had my spots that felt comforting and safe. I still don't feel like I know where much is here except for school. My mom and I don't go anywhere. I go to Ashton's occasionally. Luci and I have gotten closer, but our big outings have been school games and Henry's party.

I thought I was going to have a normal life when I moved here and went to school. Nothing about this is normal and none of it is what it seems. Even our move here was under false pretenses.

It's all too much. I don't want to be in this house or in this city. And if I don't get into Columbia, I don't have a plan B.

I need to come up with one, and fast.

My mom knocks a few hours later and Stefen sets down a large suitcase, a garment bag, and my backpack just inside the door. My mom lingers after he smiles and walks back out.

"If you need anything else, let me know and we'll go back. I tried to get the makeup I've seen you using lately."

"If someone's watching our house, don't you think they saw you come right back over here?"

"We were very cautious," is all she'll say. "And this house is safe."

"If it's so safe and ours isn't, why were we ever there? Don't trust him, Mom. Just...don't."

She gives me that long-suffering look again with the weary sigh that says I am threatening to *undo her*, and puts her hand on her hip. "You'll have to trust me this time."

I bite back my words and when she leaves, I open the suitcase. It's got more in it than I expected. My clothes are carefully folded and I open it wider, expecting to see my uniforms. Instead, it's at least a week's worth of clothes, mostly lounge clothes. Inside the garment bag are all of my uniforms, and my backpack has my laptop and the books I brought home from school. I go online and work on the day's missed assignments before I take another shower. I put on a tank and shorts and crawl into bed. I found sheets in the dresser earlier and changed the sheets, so at least I feel more removed from Raf than I did yesterday.

After I go to sleep, I wake up in the night and feel like someone is in my room. I sit up, looking around wildly. No one is there, and I reluctantly lie back, willing my heart to stop galloping in my chest. My sleep is fitful the rest of the night. When the alarm goes off the next morning, I feel like I didn't sleep at all.

CHAPTER TWENTY-ONE

I go to the kitchen hoping coffee will help and Raf is there, pouring a cup. I want to walk right back out, but I need the caffeine too much if I expect to get through the day. My mom steps in and smiles when she sees me.

"Raf agreed to take you to school today," she says. "Can I make you some breakfast? Eggs, anyone?"

"I ate already. Thanks," Raf says.

"Nothing for me. And I'll take myself to school, thank you."

"I'm not asking, I'm insisting," Mom says.

I glare at her and she flinches but stands steady, her jaw clenching.

Raf leans back against the counter, grinning, his gaze ping-ponging back and forth.

I get a mug and fill it with coffee, pouring cream inside until it's the perfect caramel shade.

"I'll be ready to go in ten minutes," Raf says.

I have to choke out the words, but I manage. "I'll drink this, brush my teeth, and then I'll be ready."

"You're not gonna do something with that?" He points to my face which is free of makeup and I fling all of that hatred toward him in my look. He doesn't flinch at all. He laughs.

My mom lifts an eyebrow at him and he shuts up. I'd laugh if I weren't so angry with both of them. I don't know why my mom is trying to ruin my life, and I don't know why Raf is either, but it's nice to see her *sort of* defend me.

I'm grasping for straws here, anything to see Raf put in his place. I put a little bit of mascara and lipstick on, but it has nothing to do with Raf.

It doesn't.

But he still smirks when he sees me like he's sure that I put it on just to make him happy. I should've left my face clean just to spite him, but I'd feel naked if I went to school without any makeup and I'd rather feel better about myself than worry about what he's assuming.

Ashton is waiting by my locker when I walk in and he holds his arms out wide when he sees me.

"I've missed you so much," he says. "You should've let me come visit," he whispers in my ear. "Everything okay at Raf's? How long are you there?"

Raf slams his locker and I can feel his eyes on us, but I'm determined to pretend he doesn't exist until he doesn't faze me anymore.

"I've missed you too." I get what I need and shut my locker. "I'm so ready to go home." This I say loud enough that I know Raf hears me, and by the way he hits the lockers as he walks by, I know it's worked.

I grin at Ashton and let out a long breath when Raf is gone.

"Fiery. I like it." Ashton laughs. He stares after Raf.

"Raf acted like he wanted to put me in the hospital. What's been going on over there?"

"Ah...just Raf trying to be in control. Not gonna happen." I feel my cheeks getting pink and try to subtly fan myself, but it doesn't work.

"Gabi? What are you not saying?"

Luci walks up then and her smile is wide. "You totally missed Raf handing Heidi her ass yesterday at lunch. It was perfect." She glances at Ashton and they laugh.

"What happened?"

"She tried to sit on his lap and he stood up and let her *fall*." She checks to see if anyone is listening. "He'd told her to get up and she ignored him." She shrugs and starts laughing again. "Her fault."

If it were anyone but Heidi and her friends I'd think it was the meanest thing ever, especially if he did sleep with her the night before...but I file it away. Nothing about Raf makes any sense.

We go to class and I make sure I'm not missing any assignments. At lunch, there's a commotion near the drinks when I walk in and I try to peer around the crowd. I get the salad, my appetite still a little weird since the craziness with my mom and my attack, and when I get closer to the drink station, a group of guys laugh around a phone. When one of them sees me, he nudges the guy next to him and they all turn to stare at me.

"What?" I look behind me to see who has their attention but it appears to be me. They shuffle until they're out of my way.

I get a drink and feel like I'm being studied inside out. My hands shake when I walk past them and my insides are jittery when I hear them erupt into another long run of laughter. I keep walking and sit down at the first table, just so I don't feel so conspicuous.

Luci finds me and sits down. "Weird table choice, but okay. Hey...what's happening with those guys?"

"Are they looking over here right now?"

"No, but Raf just hit one."

I turn around and see Raf holding a guy up by the neck before slamming him into the wall. Another guy is on the floor. The lunchroom erupts shortly after that with Ashton jumping in and hitting a guy that tries to hit Raf. Mr. Lauger and Mr. Soren get in the fray and stop the madness, dragging Raf and Ashton, along with two of the other guys, to the office.

"What the hell just happened?"

I text Ashton but he doesn't answer me. They don't come back during lunch and before I get to my next class, I'm still watching my phone every few seconds. Heidi and Amber walk by and they're laughing at something on their phone. Heidi has her head down and nearly runs right into me. When I hold out my hand to stop her, she looks up at me, her expression pure evil.

"The lady of the hour," she says before busting into a fit of uncontrollable laughter.

I've never even heard her laugh sound anything but fake before, but it's real now, so I'm curious about what has her so entertained. I hear moaning and she laughs harder, wiping her eyes.

Someone moans, "Yes," and then a guy says, "You like that, baby?"

I push the phone out of her hand and it falls to the ground, the screen shattering. Heidi starts yelling at me, shoving me back, but I barely hear her. I move around her and bend down, my focus lasered on the video playing on her phone.

I pick it up and start running and she doesn't stop me. Her laugh echoes down the hall and I can still hear her when I'm out the door. When the video is over, I play it from the beginning, and when it ends the second time, I throw up in the parking lot.

Luci finds me out there and I ask her to take me home. She doesn't ask questions. When I have her pull into my driveway, she doesn't hesitate.

"Are you okay?" she asks. "What's going on, Gabi?"

I feel cold inside.

Dead.

Hollowed out.

"I'll talk to you later, okay?" I say it so softly, she leans closer to hear me and I turn to her then, barely seeing her. "Thank you for bringing me home. I appreciate it."

"You're scaring me," she says. "I'm coming in, okay?"

"No, it's okay. I'm just not feeling well. Thank you."

I get out of the car and run into my house, slamming the door and running up the stairs to my bedroom, shutting the door behind me. Only then do I collapse on my bed and let out the grief of the horror that is my life.

The video is of Luke and me having sex in his bedroom, and it's on one of the most popular porn sites in the world.

The first time I saw Luke was at the annual Christmas party thrown by my parents. I'd never been allowed to go anywhere near the party, and this time was no exception. Usually, I got dropped off at a bookstore or occasionally went to a friend's house, but this time, I'd told my parents I was too tired to go anywhere.

I snuck down midway through the party, when the noise level had reached an impossible decibel to think about anything else. I was in my sweats and a skimpy tank, certain I wouldn't be seen, but on my way down the stairs, I saw a guy walk in the front door. He was late for the party and antsy. I thought he was nervous.

He looked up and saw me creeping down the stairs and smiled. He was the hottest guy I'd ever seen up to that point and a little younger than the other guests I'd seen walking up the driveway earlier.

I smiled back and pointed toward the noise down the hall. "The party's in there."

"Why aren't you in there?"

I smirked, flattered that he thought I was old enough to be there. I sat down on the steps and felt the heat of his stare on my legs, my chest, my face. His teeth were so white when he smiled, and when he moved closer to me, my heart started pounding.

"This looks like where the real party should be," he said.

And with that, my crush was sealed.

He stayed with me on the stairs for a couple of hours. It was the highlight of my entire life up to that point, having someone's attention on me for so long. I thought I'd found my soulmate. We talked about everything from the people at the party to life in Vegas and how we both liked penguins. He didn't leave my side. Until the party started to die down and people began to trickle out. Looking back at that night, I've wondered if he purposely left before anyone knew he was there. If he meant to hide out next to me, or if he enjoyed himself so much that he didn't care who saw us together.

The fact that we began to meet in secret not long after that should've been answer enough—I was his dirty little secret.

But, he was never fully mine.

He took my innocence and stomped on it.

After.

CHAPTER TWENTY-TWO

I grab a small suitcase from my mom's closet and haul it back to my room. Since a lot of my nice underwear is in the suitcase she packed for me already at Raf's house, there isn't much to pick from, so all that's left goes in. I throw clothes in as fast as I can, a new toothbrush, and an old mascara and lip gloss. I don't even fill it all the way before zipping it up. I'll regret leaving my laptop, but it's not a big deal. The objective is to stay light and get out of here quickly.

I'm down the stairs and at the back door when I see a note on the kitchen table. I pause next to it, heart thumping with the words torn out from a magazine and pasted on a white sheet of paper.

I know who it's from, but it would be impossible to prove.

Any promises I made are off now.

. . .

I'd recognize it as one of my father's threats any day. I'm just not sure why *now*. Stefen and my mom? Me hooking up with Raf? I don't know. But I feel uneasy as I back out of the room.

I reach the back door and jump out of my skin when I run into Raf. I scream and he holds his hand over my mouth.

"What are you doing here?" he asks, the fury in his eyes scaring me almost as much as him startling me.

"Let me go."

He doesn't listen, his grip on my arm tightening instead. "I can't. You can't be here, Gabi. It isn't safe." He picks up my suitcase and then in the next second, he hauls me over his shoulder.

"I threw up not even half an hour ago. Put me down."

"I'd rather you not throw up on me, but I'm not scared of a little mess." His voice is a deadly calm. He walks to the back of the house and goes out our gate and through his, not even slightly out of breath from the weight of me and the suitcase.

"Set me down," I yelp.

"I'll set you down when we're safely inside."

"I hate you." I kick him, hoping to get his balls but not getting so lucky.

"You're getting awfully repetitive," he says. "I think we should save those words for when we've had sex again. Otherwise, it's just monotonous."

He tosses me on the couch like I'm a bag of potatoes and stands over me, arms folded across his chest.

"We'll never have sex again so I'm saying it until it sinks in."

"You'll never be able to act like you don't want me,

Gabi. I know the truth now. I felt it in the way your pussy squeezed me like a vise."

I flush and hold up my hand. "It had been too long since I'd had sex, that's all. It meant nothing." I sit up. "Obviously."

His eyes flash and his cheeks mottle, like he's on fire within.

"I don't want to be here. The walls are closing in and this is the last place that feels safe to me."

"Okay, where could we go that would help?" he asks through gritted teeth.

I frown at him. "Why would you want to help me?"

"My father will kill me if I let you run away. That's what you were trying to do, isn't it?"

"How about you don't tell him anything and we'll call it even? I'm not going back to school. Ever." I pull my phone out of my pocket and there are twelve missed calls from Ashton.

"You don't strike me as a quitter."

"You saw the video, didn't you? That's why you were fighting..." My eyes flit up to his for a moment and it's enough. The answer is apparent. I bite my lip to keep from losing it again and avoid looking at him. I put my legs on the floor and face straight ahead. "I wish I could figure you out."

"Pretty simple. My dad wants in your mom's pants. I keep you safe, your mom is happy...my dad is happy."

Disgusted, I get up and walk to the window. Their view is even better than ours, a clearer shot of the water behind their house and even closer to the beach. Raf keeps talking, but I tune him out. As much as I hate to admit it, the hurt is deeper than I expected to feel, the way he talks about me like I'm a means to an end.

I can't think about the pain. There are too many other

hurts to knock me down right now, like the fact that what I thought was a private experience between Luke and me is all anyone will see now when they look at me.

My lips tremble and I move to open the screen door. It's locked, but I quickly figure out how to open it and slip out, while Raf is still talking. Once I'm outside, I run. Across the deck, down the steps, out the gate, and when I hit the sand, I feel like I'm on the homestretch. I vaguely hear Raf behind me, but it doesn't matter. My first steps in the water are relief. I take step after step until I'm sinking underneath the waves and let the tide pull me out.

Weightless.

The water tugs on me for a little while, but then I feel the urge to swim. It's as if I'm taken over by superhuman strength that I didn't know I had. I'm not the best swimmer, my days in Vegas mostly spent sunbathing if I ever went near a pool. We didn't have a pool, so this shouldn't feel as good as it does.

Until it doesn't.

I'm swimming, feeling like I'm owning the world and finding my freedom.

Until my strength is zapped.

I'm fine one moment and flailing the next. I forget every hurt, every wrong done against me, every pain I've felt since losing myself to Luke, who never cared about me at all. The struggle to distance myself from the feelings where Raf is concerned. Because I do...I feel so much. I feel everything.

In that moment, none of it matters.

My arms and legs are weak, and I take a huge, gulping breath, swallowing water in the process. I sink underneath the water and feel a sudden surge of peace when everything goes dark. The roar of life underneath the water is comforting and I let it sink, sink, sink with me like an anchor. I close my eyes and don't fight the lull in my body. I welcome it. I'm tired and this life is too hard. I don't want to struggle anymore. I don't want to fight to be heard, to be understood. The peace is a welcome relief and I succumb to it.

I don't know when I realize that I'm out of the cocoon of the water. If I'd known, I would've fought it harder. But it's too late when I take a deep breath and I'm on dry ground.

I keep my eyes closed, trying to get back to the solitude that is in the deep waters, but I hear an incessant beeping and feel the bright lights on me even though my eyes are tightly shut. This isn't peaceful. I feel the rush of activity around me, feel the weight that comes with knowing I will have to wake up and function in real life again. When the waves lapping around my mind cause me to drift under again, I welcome them wholeheartedly.

I feel a hand in mine before I ever open my eyes. Solid and strong. I don't give it much thought because all I want to do is go back to sleep, but the hand squeezes mine when I start to move and I know I'm breaking the surface of reality. I don't want to wake up. If I'd had my way, I would've never woken up again.

"You have to live, Gabriela. This isn't just up to you." I hear his voice, just inches next to my face, his breath hot against me. "Open your eyes, dammit."

My eyes flutter as I try to go back to the dream and yet, I

hear his words and everything in me rises against him. I fight him even in my subconscious.

I hear talking in the background. My mother. Her tears. I feel terrible for the pain I'm causing her, but not terrible enough.

"Sweetheart, wake up. Why would you do this?" My mom's tears fall on my hand and her shudders shake the bed. "Please, let us know that you're okay."

I try to sink back into that deep dark place that felt so much better than this, but it isn't coming back to me. *Why couldn't I have just drowned?*

"The doctor says to keep talking to her," Raf says. "She can most likely hear us and is aware of what's going on."

"Do you think she...wanted to die?" My mom's voice breaks and she sobs, her forehead landing on my hand as she clutches it so tight.

"No," Raf says. "She was just swimming...trying to get some exercise and forget a little bit..."

Right.

Even in my semi-comatose state, I'm challenging Raf Barron.

I'd laugh if I wasn't so angry that I'm still alive.

To read the continuing story, click here: Unspoken

ACKNOWLEDGMENTS

Huge thanks to Christine Estevez for a clean manuscript, Jena Brignola for the amazing cover, and my family for all the love.

ABOUT THE AUTHOR

When Hattie Jude is not reading, she's writing...and when she's not doing either of those things, she wishes she was.

Follow me on Facebook for book updates.

Follow me on Instagram.

Follow me on Tiktok.

Subscribe to my newsletter for up-to-date info about my books and for ARC opportunities.

instagram.com/hattiejudeauthor

.

ALSO BY HATTIE JUDE

Unwritten: https://geni.us/YHJYB

Unspoken: https://geni.us/2nzN6

The Longlake Duet: https://geni.us/meYv

Bentley: https://geni.us/pvq6Awo

Quinn: https://geni.us/B5Ch

The Love Your Enemy Duet: https://geni.us/PTyo

Traitor: https://geni.us/CjVRf

Thief: https://geni.us/ABzfAe

Lover: https://geni.us/2hSUHR

Loxley Prep series: https://geni.us/SOplJTH

Player, a Loxley Prep novel: https://geni.us/PlayerHattieJude